U0088402

雅典文化

OK,no problem!

你一定要會的基礎對話

Basic Conversation

張瑜凌 編著

CONTENTS

目錄

42

情境4

: I'm so nervous.

我好緊張喔！

: Just relax.

放鬆一下！

情境5

A: Let's talk about it later.

晚一點再聊吧！

B: Why? What's the matter?

為什麼？怎麼了？

46

情境6

A: Busy now?

你在忙嗎？

B: What can I do for you?

我能為你做什麼？

情境7

A: Is that clear?

夠清楚嗎？

B: I still have a question.

我還有一個問題！

050

情境8

A: Madam, allow me.

女士，讓我來吧！

B: I can manage it by myself.

我可以自己處理。

052

情境9

A: Thank you so much.

非常謝謝你！

B: Don't mention it.

不必客氣。

情境10

A: You've been very helpful.

你真的幫了大忙！

B: What are friends for?

朋友是幹什麼用的？

情境11

A: Forget it.

算了！

B: I don't want to know anymore.

反正我也不想要知道了！

情境12

A: Maybe next month!

也許時間就是下個月！

B: Don't even think about it.

想都別想！

060

情境13

A: Let me help you with it.

我來幫你！

B: Please don't bother.

請不必這麼麻煩。

062

情境14

A: My mistake.

都是我的錯！

B: No one blames you.

沒有人責備你！

064

情境15

A: I've brought you too much trouble.

我給你製造太多的麻煩了！

B: Let it be.

就讓它過去吧！

066

情境16

A: How could you do this to me?

你怎麼能這麼對我？

B: Don't blame me.

不要責怪我！

情境17

A: Why did you do this?

你為什麼要這樣做？

B: It wasn't me.

不是我啦！

070

情境18

A: It was you.

都是你!

B: Please. Don't tell anyone else.

拜託!不要告訴其他人!

072

情境19

A: It was all you.
全都是因為你！

B: Would you forgive me?
你願意原諒我嗎？

074

情境20

A: It's not my fault.
這不是我的錯！

B: How could you say that?
你怎麼能這麼說？

情境21

A: Can you give me a lift?
可以讓我搭便車嗎？

B: Of course.
當然可以！

078

情境22

A: I don't buy it.
我才不相信！

B: We will see.
等著瞧吧！

情境23

A: Deal?
就這麼說定了？

B: Yeah, let's have a deal.
好啊，就這麼說定了！

082

情境24

A: I give up.
我放棄！

B: Come on.
你得了吧！

084

情境25

A: I didn't break the rules.
我沒有違反規定。

B: Says who?
誰說的？

086

情境26

A: What the hell…
怎麼搞的…？

B: I don't want this.
我也不想要這樣！

情境27

A: We'll be late.
我們快要遲到了！

B: It's still early.
還很早啊！

090

情境28

A: Hurry up!
快一點！

B: I'm not ready yet.
我還沒準備好！

092

情境29

A: Come on, move on.
快一點，動作加快！

B: I heard you.
我有聽到啦！

094

情境30

A: Where did you get this?
哪裡買的？

B: It's a birthday present.
是生日禮物！

096

情境31

A: It's awesome.
真酷！

B: It's amazing.
真是令人感到訝異！

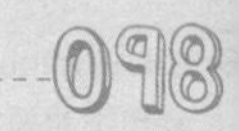

情境32

A: You'll have to pay for it.
你一定會為此事付出代價。

B: What makes you think so?
你為什麼會這麼認為？

100

情境33

A: What are you going to do?
你打算怎麼作？

B: I have no idea.
我不知道。

102

情境34

A: It's possible, isn't it?

有可能，不是嗎？

B: Could be, but I'm not so sure.

有可能，但我不確定。

104

情境35

A: Just listen to me.

聽我說！

B: It's enough.

夠了！

106

情境36

A: Stop it.

住手！

B: What did I do?

我做了什麼事？

108

情境37

A: Don't do this anymore.

不要再這麼做了！

B: It won't happen again.

我保證不會再發生！

110

情境38

A: May I use your phone?

可以借我打個電話嗎？

B: Go ahead.

去吧！

112

情境39

A: Excuse me.

借過。

B: Sure.

好啊！

114

情境40

A: Did you do this?

這是你做的嗎？

B: I did nothing.

我沒做什麼事啊！

116

情境41

A: Shall we?

可以走了嗎？

B: OK, let's go.

可以，我們走吧！

118

情境42

A: It's a perfect day for shopping.

今天很適合去逛街購物。

B: It's a good idea.

好主意！

120

情境43

A: How about some coffee?

要不要喝點咖啡？

B: Sounds good.

聽起來不錯！

122

情境44

A: It's interesting.
有趣喔！

B: Yeah, it looks great.
是啊！看起來不錯耶！

124

情境45

A: How do you like it?
你喜歡嗎？

B: I love it.
我喜歡！

126

情境46

A: It happens.
常有的事。

B: It does?
真的（經常發生）嗎？

128

情境47

A: It's so weird.
好奇怪喔！

B: It's no big deal.
這沒什麼大不了！

130

情境48

A: How are you doing?
你好嗎？

B: Pretty good.
我很好！

132

情境49

A: What's up?
近來好嗎？

B: I'm OK.
我很好！

134

情境50

A: You look sexy.
你看起來很性感。

B: Are you kidding me?
你在開我玩笑吧？

136

情境51

A: What's new?
有什麼新鮮事？

B: I got fired.
我被炒魷魚了。

138

情境52

A: You look terrible.
你看起來糟透了！

B: I'm not myself today.
我今天什麼事都不對勁！

140

情境53

A: You look upset.
你看起來很沮喪喔！

B: Don't worry about me.
不用擔心我啦！

142

情境54

A: I was having a bad day.

我今天做什麼都不太順利。

B: Really? Not surprised.

真的嗎？我一點都不訝異！

144

情境55

A: I didn't have a chance.

我沒有半點機會！

B: How come?

怎麼會呢？

146

情境56

A: How did it go?

事情順利吧？

B: Everything went well.

一切都順利！

148

情境57

A: You are the best.

你是最棒的。

B: Oh, I'm flattered.

喔！我受寵若驚。

150

情境58

A: I want to spend my life with Kenny.

我想和肯尼共度一生。

B: I'm glad to hear that.

我很高興聽你這麼說。

152

情境59

A: I have to stop smoking.

我必需要戒菸。

B: I'm really happy for you.

我真為你感到高興。

154

情境60

A: Hey, tell me your secrets.

嘿，把你的祕密告訴我吧！

B: I'm not telling.

我不會說的。

156

情境61

A: I don't know which one is better.

我不知道哪一個比較好。

B: It's your choice.

你自己決定！

158

情境62

A: You know what?

你知道嗎？

B: What?

什麼？

160

情境63

A: Don't do this.

不要這麼做！

B: Why not?

為什麼不要呢？

162

情境64

A: They don't believe you, do they?
他們不相信你，對吧？
B: How do you know?
你怎麼會知道？

164

情境65

A: I can't believe it.
我真不敢相信！
B: Easy!
放輕鬆點！

166

情境66

A: I need some fresh air.
我要呼吸一點新鮮空氣!
B: OK. Let's go for a ride.
好啊!我們開車去逛逛!

168

情境67

A: You know what I mean?
你知道我的意思嗎？
B: Got it.
我知道！

170

情境68

A: Did you get what you want?
你有拿到想要的東西了嗎？
B: Yes, I did.
有，我已經拿到了！

172

情境69

A: Check this out!

你看！

B: I see nothing.

我沒有看到有東西啊！

174

情境70

A: How was your date?

你的約會怎麼樣？

B: He stood me up again.

他又放我鴿子了。

176

情境71

A: Is it good enough?

夠好嗎？

B: Not even close.

差太遠了！

178

情境72

A: Does it really look OK?

看起來還真的不錯嗎？

B: Yeah, I think so.

是啊！我認為是如此。

180

情境73

A: By the way, I'm Kenny.

對了，我是肯尼。

B: I've heard so much about you.

久仰大名！

182

情境74

A: I used to be a singer.
我以前曾經是歌手。
B: Is that a joke?
這是開玩笑嗎？

184

情境75

A: Can I try it on?
我可以試穿嗎？
B: No problem.
可以啊！

186

情境76

A: I have something for you.
我有東西要給你！
B: It's for me?
是要給我的？

188

情境77

A: I took your advice.
我有聽你的建議！
B: Good for you.
對你來說是好的！

190

情境78

A: How do you know so much?
你怎麼會知道這麼多事？
B: It's a secret.
這是祕密！

192

情境79

A: Your name is Kenny, right?
你是肯尼對吧？

B: Yes, I am.
是的，我就是！

194

情境80

A: Can I have a look?
我可以看一下嗎？

B: I don't think so.
我不這麼認為。

196

情境81

A: I don't want to go steady.
我不想定下來。

B: I couldn't agree less.
我是絕對不會同意的。

198

情境82

A: Did you have a fight?
你們吵架啦？

B: Not really.
不盡然！

200

情境83

A: They fall in love.
他們兩人陷入熱戀了！

B: No shit!
不會吧！

202

情境84

A: It doesn't make any sense.
沒有道理啊！

B: Nobody cares!
沒人會在乎！

204

情境85

A: Look what I've got.
你看我有什麼東西！

B: Where did you get this?
你從哪裡得到這個的？

206

情境86

A: I bet it cost a fortune?
我猜這個很貴喔？

B: I will say.
的確是這樣。

208

情境87

A: What a bargain!
真是划算啊！

B: I know.
我知道啊！

210

情境88

A: What a mess over here.
這裡真是一團亂！

B: I'm terribly sorry.
我真的很抱歉！

212

情境89

A: Do you remember that?

你記得嗎？

B: I don't remember.

我不記得耶！

214

情境90

A: It'll only take you 5 minutes.

只會花你五分鐘的時間。

B: Good. This will save me a lot of time.

很好！這樣會節省我很多時間。

216

情境91

A: So glad we bumped into each other!

真高興遇到你！

B: What a small world.

世界真的很小！

218

情境92

A: Tell me more.

再多告訴我一點。

B: About what?

有關什麼事？

220

情境93

A: I'll tell you what....

你知道嗎？

B: I'm listening.

我在聽！

222

情境94

A: That doesn't sound too bad.
聽起來不會太糟糕啊！

B: Not funny.
不有趣喔！

224

情境95

A: Don't flatter yourself!
別往你自己臉上貼金。

B: Come on, it's just a joke.
拜託，開玩笑的啦！

226

情境96

A: Are you kidding me?
你是開玩笑的吧？

B: I'm serious.
我是認真的。

228

情境97

A: You can't be serious.
你不是當真的吧？

B: I meant it.
我是認真的。

230

情境98

A: You must be kidding.
你是在開玩笑的吧！

B: You never know.
世事難料喔！

232

情境99

A: No kidding?

不是開玩笑的吧！

B: I'm not really sure.

我不太清楚！

234

情境100

A: Are you sure?

你確定？

B: There is no doubt about it.

那是毫無疑問的。

236

情境101

A: What do you think of it?

你覺得如何？

B: It sucks!

爛透了！

238

情境102

A: I'm innocent.

我是無辜的。

B: So what?

那又如何？

240

情境103

A: Look what you did!

看看你做的好事！

B: I'll keep it a secret.

我會保守祕密的。

242

情境104

A: When do you want it?
你什麼時候要？

B: The sooner the better.
越快越好！

244

情境105

A: I may be wrong.
我可能錯了！

B: No wonder.
這就難怪了！

246

情境106

A: How can you say that?
你怎麼能這麼說？

B: Don't get me wrong.
不要誤會我！

248

情境107

A: I'm so embarrassed.
真的很不好意思！

B: Never mind.
沒關係啊！

250

情境108

A: Is Kenny in the office?
肯尼有在辦公室裡嗎？

B: Let me check it for you.
讓我為您查一下。

252

情境109

A: I hope you like it.
希望你喜歡。

B: I do love it.
我的確很喜歡！

254

情境110

A: I'm attracted to Kenny.
我被肯尼深深吸引了。

B: Are you crazy?
你瘋啦？

256

情境111

A: Kenny is nice to veryone.
肯尼對大家都很友善！

B: Excuse me?
你說什麼？

258

情境112

A: Do you have any plans this weekend?
你這個週末有事嗎？

B: I have other plans.
我有其他計畫了！

260

情境113

A: What do you say?
你覺得如何呢？

B: Good. But not good enough.
不錯！但不夠好！

262

情境114

A: What's on your mind?
你在想什麼呢？

B: Nothing at all.
沒事啊！

264

情境115

A: You are the boss.
你是老大，說了就算！

B: What can I say?
我能說什麼？

266

情境116

A: Can't you stay for dinner?
你不能留下來吃晚餐嗎？

B: I've got to go.
我必須要走了。

268

情境117

A: We'll be fine.
我們會沒事的。

B: I hope so.
希望是這樣！

270

情境118

A: Can you finish it by three o'clock?
你能在三點鐘前完成嗎？

B: I'll do my best.
我盡量。

272

情境119

A: It's for sure.
確定了！

B: Serious?
真的嗎？

274

情境120

A: Would you do me a favor?
你能幫我一個忙嗎？

B: I'll see what I can do.
我來看看我能幫什麼忙！

276

情境121

A: It's a long story.
說來話長。

B: Try me.
說來聽聽啊！

278

情境122

A: It's a piece of cake.
太容易了。

B: It's hard to say.
這很難說啊！

280

情境123

A: I can't afford it.
我付不起。

B: It'll all work out.
事情會有辦法解決的。

282

情境124

A: It's going to happen.
事情百分百確定了。

B: Don't ever say that again.
不要再這麼說了！

284

情境125

A: I don't know what to do.
我不知道要怎麼辦！

B: Don't panic.
不要慌張！

286

情境126

A: Is such a thing possible?
這種事可能嗎？

B: No way!
不可能！

288

情境127

A: Did anybody else see it?
還有其他人看到嗎？

B: No one saw it but me.
除了我沒以外，沒人看到。

290

情境128

A: You really don't want to see her, do you?
你真的不想見到她，對吧？

B: If possible.
如果可能的話！

292

情境129

A: Nobody told me anything.
沒人告訴我任何事。

B: I thought you knew it.
我以為你知道！

294

情境130

A: Please give me a new one.
請給我一個新的！

B: Sure, right away.
好，馬上就來。

296

情境131

A: It wasn't too bad.
不嚴重啦！

B: I agree.
我同意。

298

情境132

A: I'd like a cup of tea, please.
我要喝一杯茶，謝謝。

B: Here you are.
來，給你！

300

情境133

A: I'm so tired.
我好累喔！

B: Let's call it a day.
今天就告一個段落吧！

302

情境134

A: Let's take a break.

我們休息一會兒。

B: Time is running out!

沒有時間了！

304

情境135

A: I had a terrible hangover after the party.

在派對後，我宿醉得十分難受。

B: I can expect it.

我想也是！

306

情境136

A: Don't be such a chicken.

不要像個膽小鬼一樣！

B: I can't help it.

我無法自制啊！

308

情境137

A: It means nothing.

沒啥意義！

B: Yeah, it is.

是啊！的確如此！

310

情境138

A: It's somebody else's problem.

那是別人家的事。

B: Mind your own business.

別多管閒事！

312

情境139

A: It's not easy for you.
難為你了！

B: Could you give me an idea for it?
你能給我建議？

314

情境140

A: Can't you do anything right?
你真是成事不足，敗事有餘！

B: It's not the point.
這不是重點。

316

情境141

A: Hi, can I help you?
嗨，需要我的幫忙嗎？

B: I'm afraid not.
恐怕不可以！

318

情境142

A: And you?
你呢？

B: Coffee, please.
請給我咖啡。

320

情境143

A: Good luck to you.
祝你好運。

B: I really need it.
我真的需要有好運氣。

322

情境144

A: Got a minute?

現在有空嗎？

B: What do you want?

你想怎麼樣？！

324

情境145

A: Look at you.

看看你！

B: I don't mind.

我不在意！

326

情境146

A: I look forward to it.

我很期待這件事。

B: You will be sorry.

你會後悔的！

328

情境147

A: It's so confusing.

事情實在啟人疑竇。

B: Say no more.

不要再說了！

330

情境148

A: It's too good to be true.

哪有這麼好的事？

B: What do you mean by that?

你這是什麼意思？

332

情境149

A: It's shame on you.
你太丟臉了。

B: Leave me alone.
不要管我！

334

情境150

A: It's impossible.
不可能！

B: You can't complain.
你該知足了！

336

情境151

A: Someone has a crush on Penny.
有人對潘妮很著迷。

B: Never heard of that!
沒聽說過！

338

情境152

A: Say something.
說說話吧！

B: Don't look at me.
不要看我！

340

情境153

A: That is life.
人生就是這樣！

B: Are you done?
你說完了嗎？

342

情境154

A: Let me try.

我來試一下！

B: It's your choice.

這是你的抉擇。

344

情境155

A: Uh, no!

喔，不會吧？

B: I have no choice.

我別無選擇啊！

346

情境156

A: See? Didn't I tell you so?

看吧！我不是告訴過你嗎？

B: What shall I do now?

我現在該怎麼辦？

情境 1

Track 001

人際關係的建立就在一來一往之間，當你覺得受到某些不合理的對待時，不妨直接說出來吧！

基礎對話

A: You don't care, right?
你都不關心，對吧?

B: Whatever!
隨便你怎麼說!

深入分析

You don't care, right?
你都不關心，對吧?

若是對某事或某人毫不關心，甚至冷感時，就是不care，表示不在意的意思。

應用會話

A: You don't care, right?
你都不關心，對吧？

B: I do.
當然關心啊！

應用會話

A: You don't care, right?

你都不關心，對吧？

B: No, I don't.

沒有，我沒有啊！

深入分析

Whatever!

隨便你怎麼說！

你完全不在意對方的言論，就可以說Whatever，表示無論你說什麼都和我無關、我都無動於衷的意思。

應用會話

A: This is too much.

這太超過了！

B: Whatever!

隨便你怎麼說！

應用會話

A: I really don't want to talk about it right now.

我現在真的不想討論這件事。

B: Whatever!

隨便你怎麼說！

想要和對方聊一聊時，得要先問問對方有沒有空，以免失禮地打擾到對方喔！

基礎對話

A: Got a minute to talk?
有空談一談嗎？

B: Sure. What's up?
當然有啊！什麼事？

深入分析

Got a minute to talk?
有空談一談嗎？

希望和對方談話，就可以先問Got a minute to talk?表示這段談話只會花一分鐘的時間（a minute），或很短的時間。

應用會話

A: Got a minute to talk?
有空談一談嗎？

B: Not now, please.
拜託不要現在（談）！

應用會話

A: Got a minute to talk?

有空談一談嗎？

B: Sure. Sit down, please.

當然有啊！請坐！

深入分析

Sure. What's up?
當然啊！什麼事？

當對方提出希望談話的要求時，若你願意聊一聊，就可以問有什麼事：What's up?

應用會話

A: Busy now?

現在忙嗎？

B: Sure. What's up?

當然啊！什麼事？

應用會話

A: Would you do me a favor?

你可以幫我一個忙嗎？

B: Sure. What's up?

當然啊！什麼事？

若要對方去做某事時，就可以用祈使句的語句 " go+原形動詞 " ，表示命令的意味。

基礎對話

A: Go get it.
去拿吧！

B: Anything you say.
你說怎麼樣就怎麼樣！

深入分析

Go get it.
去拿吧！

" go+原形動詞 " 的句型是去命令或鼓勵對方句做某事，在這裡是「去拿吧」，含有要對方主動一點的意思。

應用會話

A: I'll need a new one.
我需要一個新的。

B: Go get it.
去拿吧！

應用會話

A: Can I have some bags?

可以給我一些袋子嗎？

B: Go get it.

去拿吧！

深入分析

Anything you say.

你說怎麼樣就怎麼樣！

表示對對方所說的話不在意，有任由對方自行解讀、建議或想像的意思，表示自己不評論也不辯解。

應用會話

A: You should save money.

你應該要存錢。

B: Anything you say.

你說怎麼樣就怎麼樣！

應用會話

A: Why don't we try the Red Restaurant?

為什麼我們不試試紅餐廳呢？

B: Anything you say.

你說怎麼樣就怎麼樣！

情境 4

當對方表達出某些情緒狀況時，是需要你積極回應，可以藉由兩人的互動看出彼此的交情喔！

基礎對話

A: I'm so nervous.

我好緊張喔！

B: Just relax.

放輕鬆！

深入分析

I'm so nervous.
我好緊張喔！

nervous是緊張、不安的意思，說這句話就表示自己希望對方能安撫或替你解決問題的意思。

應用會話

A: I'm so nervous.

我好緊張喔！

B: About what?

關於什麼事在緊張？

應用會話

A: I'm so nervous.
我好緊張喔！

B: Come on! Easy!
不要這樣，放輕鬆！

深入分析

Just relax.
放輕鬆！

relax是指放輕鬆，通常適用在對方情緒緊繃、無法放輕鬆時，你給予的安撫用語。

應用會話

A: Just relax.
放輕鬆！

B: I just can't.
我就是辦不到啊！

應用會話

A: Just relax.
放輕鬆！

B: OK, I will.
好，我會的！

正在談論某事時，若是需要中斷談論，就表示不想繼續話題，要適時住嘴喔！

基礎對話

A: Let's talk about it later.
晚一點再聊吧！

B: Why? What's the matter?
為什麼？怎麼了？

深入分析

Let's talk about it later.
晚一點再聊吧！

字面意思是「晚一點再談論」，其實就是表達目前自己不想再談論這件事的意思。

應用會話

A: Let's talk about it later.
晚一點再聊吧！

B: Sure.
好啊！

應用會話

A: Let's talk about it later.

晚一點再聊吧！

B: No! Tell me now.

不要，現在就告訴我！

深入分析

Why? What's the matter?

為什麼？怎麼了？

當對方發表某些言論或行為時，若你感到不解，就可以追問原因或發生何事。

應用會話

A: I feel so bored.

我好無聊！

B: Why? What's the matter?

為什麼？怎麼了？

應用會話

A: Why? What's the matter?

為什麼？怎麼了？

B: Nothing at all.

沒事啊！

情境 6

Track 006

人際間的禮貌往來就在言行之間，做任何事之前都要先確認自己不會打擾到對方喔！

基礎對話

A: Busy now?
你在忙嗎？

B: What can I do for you?
我能為你做什麼？

深入分析

Busy now?
你在忙嗎？

當你對對方有所求，或希望和對方聊一聊時，都需要先確認對方現在是不是正在忙某事。全文為 " Are you busy now? "

應用會話

A: Busy now?
你在忙嗎？

B: Nope, not at all.
沒啊，一點都不會啊！

應用會話

A: Busy now?

你在忙嗎？

B: Yeap! Leave me alone.

是啊！離我遠一點！

深入分析

What can I do for you?

我能為你做什麼？

主動提出願意協助對方的用語，不論正式或非正式場合都適用。

應用會話

A: What can I do for you?

我能為你做什麼？

B: Nothing at all.

不需要！

應用會話

A: What can I do for you?

我能為你做什麼？

B: Please pass me the salt.

請把鹽巴遞給我！

溝通是一門深奧的藝術，有道是「言者無心、聽者有意」言論難免會被誤解，得要確定彼此的認知是一致的。

基礎對話

A: Is that clear?
夠清楚嗎？

B: I still have a question.
我還有一個問題！

深入分析

Is that clear?
夠清楚嗎？

針對自己之前的言論詢問對方是否都瞭解，有主動希望對方提出問題的意思。

應用會話

A: Is that clear?
夠清楚嗎？

B: Yes, it is.
是的！

應用會話

A: Is that clear?

夠清楚嗎？

B: I don't know...

我不知道耶…

深入分析

I still have a question.

我還有一個問題！

問題發生時得要問清楚，提問之前，要先禮貌的告知自己還有問題要問！

應用會話

A: Any questions?

有任何問題嗎？

B: Yes, I still have a question.

有的，我還有一個問題！

應用會話

A: I still have a question.

我還有一個問題！

B: Shoot.

說吧！

情境 8

Track 008

現今願意主動提出協助的人不多見了，人際間的交往不再只是侷限在彼此熟識的人之間喔！

基礎對話

A: Madam, allow me.
女士，讓我來吧！

B: I can manage it by myself.
我可以自己處理。

深入分析

Madam, allow me.
女士，讓我來吧！

字面意思是「允許我...」，當發現對方正陷於某種困境時，你主動提出願意幫忙執行的意思。常見的稱呼語則有madam（女士）、sir（先生）等。

應用會話

A: Allow me, sir.
先生，讓我來吧！

B: Thanks a lot.
多謝啦！

應用會話

A: Allow me.

讓我來吧！

B: Don't worry about me.

不要擔心我啦！

深入分析

I can manage it by myself.

我可以自己處理。

你若要拒絕對方的幫忙不可以直接說no，而改成回應 " I can manage it by myself. " 也就是表示自己無須對方的協助。

應用會話

A: May I help you, sir?

先生，需要我協助嗎？

B: I can manage it by myself.

我可以自己處理。

應用會話

A: I can manage it by myself.

我可以自己處理。

B: Sure.

好吧！

人際關係需要經營，當接受他人的幫助時，不要吝嗇道謝。

基礎對話

A: Thank you so much.
　非常謝謝你！

B: Don't mention it.
　不必客氣。

深入分析

Thank you so much.
非常謝謝你！

說謝謝有很多程度的不同，一般是Thank you（謝謝）就可以，若是「非常感謝」，則可以說Thank you so much.非正式場合則可以說Thanks或Thanks a lot.（多謝）

應用會話

A: Thank you so much.
　非常謝謝你！

B: You are welcome.
　不必客氣！

應用會話

A: Let me help you with it.

我來幫你！

B: Thank you so much.

非常謝謝你！

深入分析

Don't mention it.
不必客氣。

對方若道謝，你也不要忘記回應對方「不必客氣」：Don't mention it.也可以說It's OK或No problem。You are welcome.則是正式場合的用法。

應用會話

A: Thank you very much.

非常感謝。

B: Don't mention it.

不必客氣。

應用會話

A: Thanks.

謝啦！

B: Don't mention it.

不必客氣。

互助是人類最高的情操之一，當接受對方的幫助時，除了謝謝 (Thank you) 之外，你還可以如何回應呢？

基礎對話

A: You've been very helpful.
你真的幫了大忙！

B: What are friends for?
朋友是幹什麼用的？

深入分析

You've been very helpful.
你真的幫了大忙！

直接說明對方的所作所為是很有幫助的，雖沒有Thank you的字眼，卻也是表達謝意的一種方式。

應用會話

A: You've been very helpful.
你真的幫了大忙！

B: I have?
我有嗎？

應用會話

A: You've been very helpful.

你真的幫了大忙！

B: No problem.

不必客氣！

深入分析

What are friends for?

朋友是幹什麼用的？

當對方感謝你的協助，你除了可以制式化說「不必客氣」（You are welcome），也可以說What are friends for?帶有中文「兩肋插刀」的協助豪氣。

應用會話

A: I really appreciate it.

我真的很感恩！

B: What are friends for?

朋友是幹什麼用的？

應用會話

A: What are friends for?

朋友是幹什麼用的？

B: Good to hear that.

很高興聽你這麼說。

情境 11

人際間並不是都很順遂的，如果彼此之間發生一些誤會，該如何回應才可以表示自己的不悅呢？

基礎對話

A: Forget it.
算了！

B: I don't want to know anymore.
反正我也不想要知道了！

深入分析

Forget it.
算了！

forget it字面意思是「忘記」，卻是可能是自己想要說的話被打斷、被誤解時，你不願再追究或放棄時的用語，表示自己不想再提及或解釋之意。

應用會話

A: What's the cause of the delay?
是什麼原因延誤？

B: Forget it.
算了！

應用會話

A: Forget it.

算了！

B: Come on, let's have a talk.

不要這樣，我們談談吧！

深入分析

I don't want to know anymore.

反正我也不想要知道了！

對方試圖解釋，但已經引不起你的興趣時，可以直接挑明的說I don't want to know anymore.表示自己知不知道已經無所謂了！

應用會話

A: Do you want to know the truth?

想不想知道實情？

B: I don't want to know anymore.

反正我也不想要知道了！

應用會話

A: Come on, you'll get over it.

好了，你熬過來的。

B: I don't want to know anymore.

反正我也不想要知道了！

Track 012

彼此正在討論事情時，當下的氣氛如何，就看你如何回應對方囉！

基礎對話

A: Maybe next month!
也許時間就是下個月！

B: Don't even think about it.
想都別想！

深入分析

Maybe next month!
也許時間就是下個月！

" maybe+名詞 " 可以表示建議或推測的意思。這句Maybe next month!是表示時間是在下個月，next month可以用其他時間替代，例如Maybe tonight、Maybe tomorrow...等。

應用會話

A: Maybe next month!
也許時間就是下個月！

B: Maybe!
或許吧！

應用會話

A: Maybe next month!

也許時間就是下個月！

B: Are you sure?

你肯定嗎？

深入分析

Don't even think about it.

想都別想！

當對方說了某事或下了某個決定，但你認為不可能或不可行時，就可以說Don't even think about it.表示要對方放棄、想都別想的意思。

應用會話

A: It's time to tell her the truth.

是該告訴她真相的時候了。

B: Don't even think about it.

想都別想！

應用會話

A: I want to see the film again.

我真想再看一遍這部電影。

B: Don't even think about it.

想都別想！

互助是優良的人際關係，當有人需要幫助時，就可以彼此互相協助、互動。

基礎對話

A: Let me help you with it.
我來幫你！

B: Please don't bother.
請不必這麼麻煩。

深入分析

Let me help you with it.
我來幫你！

help someone with it是慣用語，表示協助某人做某事的意思。it雖沒有說明是何事，但通常是對方手上正在忙的事。

應用會話

A: Let me help you with it.
我來幫你！

B: Thank you so much.
謝謝你。

A: Let me help you with it.

我來幫你！

B: No, thanks.

不用，謝啦！

深入分析

Please don't bother.
請不必這麼麻煩。

當對方提出願意幫忙，但你不願意接受協助時，就可以婉轉地回應Please don't bother.表示「不必麻煩你了」，也就是拒絕接受對方的協助。

應用會話

A: Allow me.

我來幫你！

B: Please don't bother.

請不必這麼麻煩。

應用會話

A: Come on, let me help you.

不要這樣，我來幫你吧！

B: Please don't bother.

請不必這麼麻煩。

情境 14

Track 014

當錯誤發生時，究竟應該如何面對呢？千萬不要推卸責任或得理不饒人喔！

基礎對話

A: My mistake.
都是我的錯！

B: No one blames you.
沒有人責備你！

深入分析

My mistake.
都是我的錯！

當你發覺原來是自己犯錯時，一定要在第一時間就承認錯誤喔！千萬不要因為害怕承認錯誤而掩飾自己的過錯！

應用會話

A: My mistake.
都是我的錯！

B: Yes, it is.
的確是！

應用會話

A: Hey, watch out.

嘿，小心點！

B: Oh, my mistake.

喔！都是我的錯！

深入分析

No one blames you.
沒有人責備你！

當對方道歉、承認錯誤時，你也不要過度責備對方，適時安慰對方反而能讓對方更能記取教訓。

應用會話

A: I'm very sorry about that.

為此我很抱歉。

B: No one blames you.

沒有人責備你！

應用會話

A: I just knew it. It was my fault.

我就知道！是我的錯！

B: No one blames you.

沒有人責備你！

能夠原諒別人才是人性的美德，當對方乞求你的諒解時，要如何回應呢？

基礎對話

A: I've brought you too much trouble.
我給你製造太多的麻煩了！

B: Let it be.
就讓它過去吧！

深入分析

I've brought you too much trouble.
我給你製造太多的麻煩了！

若是自己為對方造成很多困擾，就應該致歉，不一定要說sorry才是道歉，說明自己製造了很多的trouble也是致歉的方式。造成某人困擾常用bring someone trouble的句型。

應用會話

A: I've brought you too much trouble.
我給你製造太多的麻煩了！

B: It's OK.
沒關係！

應用會話

A: I've brought you too much trouble.

我給你製造太多的麻煩了！

B: So what are you gonna do?

所以你打算怎麼辦？

深入分析

Let it be.

就讓它過去吧！

當發生令人感到傷心、難過、不堪等不好的事，你就可以安慰對方Let it be.表示雲淡風清，不要再放在心上的意思。

應用會話

A: Let it be.

就讓它過去吧！

B: Well... I don't know...

嗯…我不知道耶…

應用會話

A: I can't believe it happened to me.

我不敢相信這事會發生在我身上。

B: Let it be.

就讓它過去吧！

當兩人產生爭執時，彼此之間的火藥味可就很重，此時該如何應對，正考驗著兩人的EQ喔！

基礎對話

A: How could you do this to me?
你怎麼能這麼對我？

B: Don't blame me.
不要責怪我！

深入分析

How could you do this to me?
你怎麼能這麼對我？

當對方做了對不起你的事，你是可以理直氣壯的質問對方：How could you do this to me?

應用會話

A: How could you do this to me?
你怎麼能這麼對我？

B: Sorry, I don't know.
對不起，我不知道！

應用會話

A: How could you do this to me?

你怎麼能這麼對我？

B: I can't help it.

我情不自禁啊！

深入分析

Don't blame me.
不要責怪我！

可能是自己所造成的錯誤，但是有時自己也是力不從心或不是有意的作為，你就可以大聲疾呼：不要怪我啊！

應用會話

A: It's all your fault.

都是你的錯！

B: Don't blame me.

不要責怪我！

應用會話

A: Don't blame me.

不要責怪我！

B: I won't.

我不會！

情境 17

Track 017

人際之間難免會產生紛爭，當這種誤解、爭吵的紛爭發生，雙方一定要靜下心來好好面對。

基礎對話

A: Why did you do this?
你為什麼要這樣做？

B: It wasn't me.
不是我啦！

深入分析

Why did you do this?
你為什麼要這樣做？

質疑對方為何要做某事的意思，因為是過去所做的事，所以通常使用過去式句型did所引導的問句。

應用會話

A: Why did you do this?
你為什麼要這樣做？

B: It's a long story.
說來話長！

應用會話

A: Why did you do this?

你為什麼要這樣做？

B: I can't help it.

我情不自禁。

深入分析

It wasn't me.

不是我啦！

表示自己被誤解了，甚至為此揹了黑鍋，就可以用這句話It wasn't me.捍衛自己的名聲。

應用會話

A: Your fault.

都是你的錯！

B: It wasn't me.

不是我啦！

應用會話

A: It wasn't me.

不是我啦！

B: Who else?

那還會有誰？

情境 18

「若要人不知，除非己莫為」，面對可能要曝光的不光彩事件，會是如何面對呢？

基礎對話

A: It was you.
都是你！

B: Please. Don't tell anyone else.
拜託！不要告訴其他人！

深入分析

It was you.
都是你！

表示彼此所認知的某事是對方所造成的，就可以嚴厲斥責對方：It was you，表示對方就是罪魁禍首，要承擔責任。

應用會話

A: It was you.
都是你！

B: No, not me.
不，不是我！

應用會話

A: It was you.

都是你！

B: I'm really sorry.

我真的很抱歉！

深入分析

Don't tell anyone else.

不要告訴其他人！

若希望對方能為自己保守祕密，就是不要告訴其他人，英文就叫做Don't tell anyone else.。

應用會話

A: Don't tell anyone else.

不要告訴其他人！

B: I won't.

我不會的！

應用會話

A: Don't tell anyone else.

不要告訴其他人！

B: Why not?

為什麼不可以？

明知對方是罪魁禍首，該如何表示自己的不滿？而罪過的一方是否願意認錯呢？

基礎對話

A: It was all you.
全都是因為你！

B: Would you forgive me?
你願意原諒我嗎？

深入分析

It was all you.
全都是因為你！

不管是直接或間接因素，目前已發生的這一切的因果，都要由對方承擔的質問語，就可以說It was all you.。

應用會話

A: It was all you.
全都是因為你！

B: So what? It's no big deal.
那又如何？這沒什麼大不了啊！

應用會話

A: It was all you.

全都是因為你！

B: I don't care.

我不在意。

深入分析

Would you forgive me?
你願意原諒我嗎？

祈求原諒最直接的用語就是forgive someone，更謙卑的祈求對方諒解則是Would you forgive me?

應用會話

A: Would you forgive me?

你願意原諒我嗎？

B: I don't give a shit.

我不在意。

應用會話

A: I can't believe it.

真教人不敢相信！

B: Would you forgive me?

你願意原諒我嗎？

當某一方為自己辯解，表示可能彼此之間是有誤會的，那麼就該釐清事情的真相到底為何！

基礎對話

A: It's not my fault.
這不是我的錯！
B: How could you say that?
你怎麼能這麼說？

深入分析

It's not my fault.
這不是我的錯！

沒有人願意被誤會，也不要為此而揹黑鍋，不是自己造成的錯誤，就應該替自己洗刷被冤枉的罪名。

應用會話

A: It's not my fault.
這不是我的錯！
B: So it's mine?
所以是我的錯囉？

應用會話

A: It's not my fault.
這不是我的錯！

B: Don't worry about it.
不要擔心！

深入分析

How could you say that?
你怎麼能這麼說？

當對方發表某些令人不解的言論時，你就可以質疑對方為何要如此說。

應用會話

A: How could you say that?
你怎麼能這麼說？

B: I don't know what to say.
我不知道該說什麼！

應用會話

A: I can't believe what you just said.
我真不敢相信你剛剛的言論！

B: How could you say that?
你怎麼能這麼說？

既然大家都順路，就可以一起搭便車喔，為地球的環保盡一份心力喔！

基礎對話

A: Can you give me a lift?
可以讓我搭便車嗎？

B: Of course.
當然可以！

深入分析

Can you give me a lift?
可以讓我搭便車嗎？

give someone a lift是提供給某人搭便車的意思，適用在你開車免費讓對方搭一程的情境。

應用會話

A: Can you give me a lift?
可以讓我搭便車嗎？

B: Sure. Where are you going?
好啊！你要去哪裡？

應用會話

A: Can you give me a lift?

可以讓我搭便車嗎？

B: No, I don't think so.

不，我不這麼認為！

深入分析

Of course.

當然可以！

當你要回答「願意」、「可以」這種正面的回應用語時，除了yes之外，也可以用Of course.替代，表示理所當然的意思。

應用會話

A: Can I go camping with my friends?

我可以和我的朋友去露營嗎？

B: Of course.

當然可以！

應用會話

A: May I leave a message?

我可以留言嗎？

B: Of course.

當然可以！

情境 22

有些人講話喜歡誇大，面對這種情境，該如何應對呢？

基礎對話

A: I don't buy it.
我才不相信！

B: We will see.
等著瞧吧！

深入分析

I don't buy it.

我不相信！

這句話並不是「我不買」，而是「我不相信」的意思，適用在對方的言行舉止或面對的情境都讓你無法相信時使用。

應用會話

A: I don't buy it.
我不相信！

B: Oh, come on.
喔！少來了！

應用會話

A: I don't buy it.

我不相信！

B: Neither do I.

我也不相信！

深入分析

We will see.

等著瞧吧！

這句並不是真的有「看」的意味，而是中文「走著瞧」，表示狀況還很難定論，要看後續的發展的意思。

應用會話

A: I don't believe it.

我才不相信。

B: We will see.

等著瞧吧！

應用會話

A: Don't you think he's gentle?

你不覺得他很有紳士風範嗎？

B: We will see.

等著瞧吧！

情境
23

Track 023

兩人之間有沒有共識很重要，如何用簡單句子來確認達成共識？

基礎對話

A: Deal?

就這麼說定了？

B: Yeah, let's have a deal.

好啊，就這麼說定了！

深入分析

Deal?

就這麼說定了？

不知道對方是否願意就彼此討論的事達成協議，所以要再Deal?確認一下！

應用會話

A: Deal?

就這麼說定了？

B: Of course.

當然！

應用會話

A: Deal?

就這麼說定了？

B: Says who?

誰說的？

深入分析

Yeah, let's have a deal.

好啊，就這麼說定了！

表示同意對方所提的建議，帶有「大家說好了，不能反悔」的意思。

應用會話

A: I don't want this.

我也不想要這樣！

B: Yeah, let's have a deal.

好啊，就這麼說定了！

應用會話

A: You promise?

你能保證嗎？

B: Yeah, let's have a deal.

好啊，就這麼說定了！

當面對無以為繼、令人沮喪的狀況時，你還會願意排除萬難持續下去嗎？

基礎對話

A: I give up.

我放棄！

B: Come on.

你得了吧！

深入分析

I give up.

我放棄！

「放棄」的確不是一個很好的態度，但是當你不得不這麼做時，雙手一攤，只好give up了！give up也帶有「不願意」的意味。

應用會話

A: I give up.

我放棄！

B: Hey, what's going on?

嘿，發生什麼事了？

應用會話

A: Coming or not?

要不要一起去？

B: I give up.

我不去！

深入分析

Come on.

你得了吧！

當對方的言行似乎是開玩笑時，你可以回應Come on，表示「你少來了」，若是在鼓勵的情境下，則有為對方打氣的意味。

應用會話

A: It's not what I mean.

我不是這個意思。

B: Come on.

你得了吧！

應用會話

A: Come on.

你得了吧！

B: I meant it.

我是認真的。

當你為自己申訴辯解時，若是對方仍舊不相信，彼此該如何應對呢？

基礎對話

A: I didn't break the rules.
我沒有違反規定。

B: Says who?
誰說的？

深入分析

I didn't break the rules.
我沒有違反規定。

break the rules字面意思是「打破規則」，也就是違反規定、違法的意思。

應用會話

A: I didn't break the rules.
我沒有違反規定。

B: Why not?
怎麼會沒有？

應用會話

A: I didn't break the rules.

我沒有違反規定。

B: Oh, I don't think so.

是嗎？我不相信！

深入分析

Says who?

誰說的？

針對對方的言論你感到不可思議或不相信時，不但要進一步追問這是誰說的，也可以藉此強化你不相信的立場。

應用會話

A: Says who?

誰說的？

B: It's Steve.

就是史帝夫啊！

應用會話

A: You don't believe it, do you?

你不相信，對吧？

B: Says who?

誰說的？

適用在當面對混亂、不可思議的事件時，一方不滿、另一方又急著為自己辯解的情境。

基礎對話

A: What the hell...

怎麼搞的…？

B: I don't want this.

我也不想要這樣！

深入分析

What the hell...

怎麼搞的…？

hell是地獄的意思，這句話沒有說完，但表示當你看到某種混亂的狀態時，想要有人解釋是怎麼回事的意思。

應用會話

A: What the hell...

怎麼搞的…？

B: Please forgive me.

請原諒我！

應用會話

A: What the hell...

怎麼搞的…？

B: Not me.

不是我啦！

深入分析

I don't want this.

我也不想要這樣！

表示這些狀況都不是自己願意見到的，甚至有「發生這樣的狀況，我也是不得已」的意思。

應用會話

A: You'd better have a good reason.

你最好有一個好的理由。

B: I don't want this.

我也不想要這樣！

應用會話

A: I don't want this.

我也不想要這樣！

B: Whatever.

隨便你怎麼樣！

時間稍縱即逝，當急驚風遇到慢郎中時，兩人的步調可是無法一致的！

基礎對話

A: We'll be late.

我們快要遲到了！

B: It's still early.

還很早啊！

深入分析

We'll be late.

我們快要遲到了！

表示快要面臨遲到的狀況，藉此提醒對方動作加速的意思。

應用會話

A: We'll be late.

我們快要遲到了！

B: OK, let's go.

好，我們出發吧！

應用會話

A: We'll be late.

我們快要遲到了！

B: I'm not ready yet.

我還沒準備好！

深入分析

It's still early.

還很早啊！

表示時間還很多，可以慢慢來、不要著急的意思。

應用會話

A: It's still early.

還很早啊！

B: Early? It's ten-thirty now.

還早？現在十點卅分了！

應用會話

A: It's still early.

還很早啊！

B: So what? I don't mind at all.

那又怎樣？我一點都不在意！

當一方準備好，另一方卻還是慢條斯理時，兩人該如何協調彼此的步調呢？

基礎對話

A: Hurry up!
快一點！

B: I'm not ready yet.
我還沒準備好！

深入分析

Hurry up!

快一點！

催促對方動作加快的直接用語，表示命令的意味。

應用會話

A: Hurry up!
快一點！

B: We've got plenty of time.
我們的時間還很多啊！

應用會話

A: Hurry up!

快一點！

B: OK! Let's move on.

好了！我們行動吧！

深入分析

I'm not ready yet.
我還沒準備好！

直接說明自己還沒有準備好，希望對方再給自己多一點的時間。

應用會話

A: Shall we?

可以走了嗎？

B: I'm not ready yet.

我還沒準備好！

應用會話

A: I'm not ready yet.

我還沒準備好！

B: It's OK. Take your time.

沒關係！你慢慢來！

彼此對時間的認知不同時，一方的催促在另一方聽起來，可是會令人不耐煩的。

基礎對話

A: Come on, move on.

快一點，動作加快！

B: I heard you.

我有聽到啦！

深入分析

Come on, move on.

快一點，動作加快！

急促的用語，要對方趕緊行動（move on）的意思。

應用會話

A: Come on, move on.

快一點，動作加快！

B: Yes, sir.

好的，長官！

應用會話

A: Come on, move on.

快一點，動作加快！

B: But I'm not feeling well...

可是我人不太舒服⋯

深入分析

I heard you.

我有聽到啦！

表示對方說的話自己已經聽到了，不要再繼續叨念，有點不耐煩的意味。

應用會話

A: Hey, are you with me?

喂，你有在聽嗎？

B: I heard you.

我有聽到啦！

應用會話

A: I heard you.

我有聽到啦！

B: You did?

你有嗎？

看到新鮮貨大家都有興趣，這也是關心對方的一種表現喔！

基礎對話

A: Where did you get this?
哪裡買的？

B: It's a birthday present.
是生日禮物！

深入分析

Where did you get this?
哪裡買的？

一般來說，get是「得到」的意思，但在Where did you get this?的句子中，則可以適用買、得到、獲取的意思。

應用會話

A: Wow! Where did you get this?
哇！哪裡買的？

B: I bought it in Taiwan.
我在台灣買的。

應用會話

A: Check this out.

你看！

B: Cool. Where did you get this?

真酷！哪裡買的？

深入分析

It's a birthday present.
是生日禮物！

表示這個物品是自己的生日禮物，但沒有說明是誰送的。若要說明是誰送的，則在後面加上 " from somewhere " 即可。

應用會話

A: What is this?

這是什麼？

B: It's a birthday present.

是生日禮物！

應用會話

A: It's a birthday present from my wife.

是我太太送的生日禮物！

B: It's so... you know... so ugly.

真的好…你知道…好醜！

當遇到令人稱羨的情境時，一句簡單的句子就足以表達酷炫的意思。

基礎對話

A: It's awesome.
　真酷！

B: It's amazing.
　真是令人感到訝異！

深入分析

It's awesome.
真酷！

awesome類似中文「酷斃」的意思，表示自己很讚賞的意思。

應用會話

A: How do you like it?
　你喜歡嗎？

B: It's awesome.
　真酷！

應用會話

A: It's awesome.

真酷！

B: You really think so?

你真的這麼認為？

深入分析

It's amazing.
真是令人感到訝異！

amazing適用在令人感到訝異、不可思議的情境，通常是屬於正面情緒的訝異表示。

應用會話

A: How do you like it?

你喜歡嗎？

B: Are you kidding? It's amazing.

你是在開玩笑吧？真是令人感到訝異！

應用會話

A: Look! It's my birthday present.

看！這是我的生日禮物！

B: Wow, it's amazing.

哇！真是令人感到訝異！

情境 32

Track 032

明知不可為而為之，當面對這樣令人擔心的情境，該如何提出警告？

基礎對話

A: You'll have to pay for it.
你一定會為此事付出代價。

B: What makes you think so?
你為什麼會這麼認為？

深入分析

You'll have to pay for it.
你一定會為此事付出代價。

提醒對方任何行為都要三思。pay是「花費」，在此暗喻對方將會為此付出慘痛的代價。

應用會話

A: You'll have to pay for it.
你一定會為此事付出代價。

B: We'll see.
我們看著辦吧！

應用會話

A: You'll have to pay for it.

你一定會為此事付出代價。

B: Give me a break.

饒了我吧！

深入分析

What makes you think so?

你為什麼會這麼認為？

當對方提出某一種言論時，你不直接表示否定的立場，而是質疑對方為何會有此想法。

應用會話

A: What makes you think so?

你為什麼會這麼認為？

B: Don't you think so?

你不這樣認為嗎？

應用會話

A: What makes you think so?

你為什麼會這麼認為？

B: Because it's getting late.

因為越來越晚了！

當對方面對為難的情境時，你可以提出自己的關心，以表示你的擔憂。

基礎對話

A: What are you going to do?
你打算怎麼作？

B: I have no idea.
我不知道。

深入分析

What are you going to do?
你打算怎麼作？

想要知道對方作何打算，也就是下一步會如何處理的意思。

應用會話

A: What are you going to do?
你打算怎麼作？

B: It depends on the situation.
要視情況而定。

應用會話

A: What are you going to do?

你打算怎麼作？

B: You tell me.

你說呢？

深入分析

I have no idea.

我不知道。

「不知道」的說法很多種，最簡單的是I don't know。而I have no idea則表示沒有想法，也就是「不知道，所以沒有想法」的意思。

應用會話

A: What do you say?

你覺得如何呢？

B: I have no idea.

我不知道。

應用會話

A: What would you recommend?

你有什麼意見？

B: I have no idea.

我不知道。

情境 34

Track 034

面對瞬息萬變的情境，各種狀況都可能發生，但很多人都不知道該如何回應。

基礎對話

A: It's possible, isn't it?
有可能，不是嗎？

B: Could be, but I'm not so sure.
有可能，但是我不確定。

深入分析

It's possible, isn't it?
有可能，不是嗎？

表示這是可能的現象，並反問對方是否同意的意思。

應用會話

A: It's possible, isn't it?
有可能，不是嗎？

B: I know.
我知道啊！

應用會話

A: It's possible, isn't it?

有可能，不是嗎？

B: It's what I meant.

我就是這個意思。

深入分析

Could be, but I'm not so sure.
有可能，但是我不確定。

回應對方這是可能的狀況，但是自己卻無法百分百確認的意思。

應用會話

A: Could be, but I'm not so sure.

有可能，但是我不確定。

B: This is great.

很好！

應用會話

A: Could be, but I'm not so sure.

有可能，但是我不確定。

B: I see.

我瞭解了！

當被誤解時，該如何為自己辯解呢？千萬不要莫名其妙就揹上黑鍋喔！

基礎對話

A: Just listen to me.
聽我說！

B: It's enough.
夠了！

深入分析

Just listen to me.
聽我說！

當你希望對方能聽聽你的解釋，就可以說Listen to me，表示希望對方給自己一個解釋說明的機會。

應用會話

A: Just listen to me.
聽我說！

B: No, stop talking to me.
不要，不要和我說話了！

應用會話

A: Just listen to me.

聽我說！

B: What? What do you want to say?

是什麼事？你想要說什麼？

深入分析

It's enough.

夠了！

當你受夠了對方，不願再看到或面臨目前的狀況，就可以說enough，表示希望對方停止目前所有的這一切言論或行為的意思。

應用會話

A: It's not what I said...

我不是這樣說的…

B: It's enough.

夠了！

應用會話

A: Would you forgive me?

你願意原諒我嗎？

B: It's enough.

夠了！

情境
36

Track 036

爭執的兩人不會只有口頭上的爭論，有時難免會有行為上的侵犯，此時就適用以下的對話。

基礎對話

A: Stop it.
住手！

B: What did I do?
我做了什麼事？

深入分析

Stop it.
住手！

希望對方能馬上停止或住手，就可以說Stop it，表示言行都就此打住的意思。

應用會話

A: Stop it.
住手！

B: I did nothing.
我什麼事都沒做啊！

應用會話

A: Stop it.

住手！

B: I can't.

我辦不到！

深入分析

What did I do?

我做了什麼事？

當你不知自己是否曾經做過何事時，就可以說What did I do?通常用過去式句型表示。

應用會話

A: What did I do?

我做了什麼事？

B: Nothing.

沒事啊！

應用會話

A: Hey, look what you did.

嘿，看你幹了什麼好事！

B: What? What did I do?

什麼啊？我做了什麼事？

發生爭執時，吵架無法解決事情，應盡速達成協議。

基礎對話

A: Don't do this anymore.

不要再這麼做了！

B: It won't happen again.

我保證不會再發生！

深入分析

Don't do this anymore.

不要再這麼做了！

表示對方做了某事，而你希望對方不要再這麼做的意思。

應用會話

A: Don't do this anymore.

不要再這麼做了！

B: Why not?

為什麼不要？

應用會話

A: Don't do this anymore.

不要再這麼做了！

B: I have no choice.

我別無選擇啊！

深入分析

It won't happen again.

我保證不會再發生！

你向對方保證，目前的情形將來不會再發生了，也適用你的言論或行為不再發生的保證。

應用會話

A: I warned you.

我警告過你了。

B: It won't happen again.

我保證不會再發生！

應用會話

A: It won't happen again.

我保證不會再發生！

B: I hope so.

希望是這樣。

情境
38

Track 038

提出需求以及回應的雙方，是可以用一種輕鬆的方式對話。

基礎對話

A: May I use your phone?
可以借我打個電話嗎？

B: Go ahead.
可以！

深入分析

May I use your phone?
可以借我打個電話嗎？

要向對方借電話使用可不是用borrow（借用）這個單字，而是直接使用use（使用）即可。

應用會話

A: May I use your phone?
可以借我打個電話嗎？

B: No, you may not.
不行！

應用會話

A: May I use your phone?

可以借我打個電話嗎？

B: Sure.

好啊！

深入分析

Go ahead.

可以！

go ahead除了可以表示往前直走，還含有答應、繼續某種行為或言論的意思，通常適用在回應的語句中。

應用會話

A: Can I go to her home and stay the night?

我可以去她家過夜嗎？

B: Go ahead.

去吧！

應用會話

A: I need your help.

我需要你的協助。

B: Go ahead.

說吧！

情境 39

Track 039

當不得已必須打擾對方時，彼此該如何面對這樣的狀況呢?

基礎對話

A: Excuse me.
借過。

B: Sure.
好啊！

深入分析

Excuse me.
借過。

當你希望對方挪出空間讓你通行時，中文會說「借過」，英文就說Excuse me。或是要打擾對方、請對方停下目前的動作聽自己說話時，都可以說Excuse me。Excuse me也有借問的意思。

應用會話

A: Excuse me.
借過。

B: No problem.
沒問題！

應用會話

A: Excuse me.

抱歉打擾一下！

B: Yes?

請說！

深入分析

Sure.

好啊！

同意的回應語除了yes或of course之外，也可簡單地說sure表示「當然好」的意思。

應用會話

A: May I have the bill, please?

請給我帳單好嗎？

B: Sure.

好的！

應用會話

A: Let me have a look.

我看一下。

B: Sure.

好啊！

情境 40

Track 040

要抓出是誰的傑作，確認的動作可是不能馬虎啊！

基礎對話

A: Did you do this?
這是你做的嗎？

B: I did nothing.
我沒做什麼事啊！

深入分析

Did you do this?
這是你做的嗎？

當你猜測某人可能做了某事時，可以用過去式的句型確認對方是不是就是做了某事（do this）的當事人。

應用會話

A: Did you do this?
這是你做的嗎？

B: No, it wasn't me.
不，不是我！

應用會話

A: Did you do this?

這是你做的嗎？

B: Yes, I did.

是的，就是我！

深入分析

I did nothing.

我沒做什麼事啊！

do nothing字面意思是「做沒事」，也就是「沒有作為」，I did nothing就表示我什麼事都沒做的意思。

應用會話

A: It was you.

就是你！

B: I did nothing.

我沒做什麼事啊！

應用會話

A: I did nothing.

我沒做什麼事啊！

B: Don't worry. It doesn't matter.

別擔心！不要緊的！

情境
41

Track 041

準備好要動身出發了嗎？不要忘記還要問問相關人，是不是可以出門了！

基礎對話

A: Shall we?
可以走了嗎？

B: OK, let's go.
可以，我們走吧！

深入分析

Shall we?
可以走了嗎？

當你要和其他人一起出門，就可以問問對方「可以走了嗎？」此時只要說Shall we?就可以，也帶有催促對方「我們準備要出發了，請快一點」的意思。

應用會話

A: Shall we?
可以走了嗎？

B: But I'm not ready yet.
但是我還沒準備好！

應用會話

A: Shall we?

可以走了嗎？

B: We're not going to wait for Kenny?

我們沒有要等肯尼嗎？

深入分析

OK, let's go.

可以，我們走吧！

let's go可以是吆喝「大家一起行動」的意思，前面先說OK,...可以是「我準備好了」，但有時也是隨口回應，並無特別的意思。

應用會話

A: OK, let's go.

可以，我們走吧！

B: Sure. Let me get a coat.

好的！讓我拿件外套。

應用會話

A: Ready?

準備好了嗎？

B: OK, let's go.

可以，我們走吧！

對方提出建議，你可以就實際的狀況回應自己的意見。

基礎對話

A: It's a perfect day for shopping.
今天很適合去逛街購物。

B: It's a good idea.
好主意！

深入分析

It's a perfect day for shopping.
今天很適合去逛街購物。

a perfect day for...表示是適合作某事的日子，for後面通常接名詞或動名詞，表示做某事的意思。

應用會話

A: It's a perfect day for shopping.
今天很適合去逛街購物。

B: Sounds good.
聽起來不錯！

應用會話

A: It's a perfect day for swimming.

今天很適合去游泳。

B: Not for me.

不適合我去。

深入分析

It's a good idea.
好主意！

當對方提出意見時，你若覺得可行，通常要禮貌的回應：It's a good idea.也可以只是說good idea表示。

應用會話

A: It's a good idea.

好主意！

B: You think so?

你真這樣認為嗎？

應用會話

A: Can I invite Jenny?

我可以邀請珍妮嗎？

B: Oh, it's a good idea.

喔，好主意！

提出建議是很常見的對話主題，該如何提出建議？又該如何回應呢？

基礎對話

A: How about some coffee?
要不要喝點咖啡？

B: Sounds good.
聽起來不錯！

深入分析

How about some coffee?
要不要喝點咖啡？

How about...是很常見的提出建議的句型，about後面通常會接名詞或動名詞，表示所提出的建議內容。

應用會話

A: How about some coffee?
要不要喝點咖啡？

B: I'd love to.
好啊！

應用會話

A: How about a cup of tea?

要不要喝杯茶？

B: No, thanks.

不，謝謝。

深入分析

Sounds good.

聽起來不錯！

若你認同對方提出的建議，除了可以說good idea（好主意）之外，還可以說sounds good表示聽起來很不錯的意思，全文的說法是It sounds good.

應用會話

A: I can fix it for you.

我可以幫你修理！

B: Sounds good.

聽起來不錯！

應用會話

A: We should do some exercise after work.

也許我們應該在下班之後做一些運動！

B: It sounds good.

聽起來不錯！

情境 44

Track 044

人際間的互動是需要經營的，不吝讚美是原則之一。當有某種建議、想法或行為很棒時，雙方該如何應對？

基礎對話

A: It's interesting.

有趣喔！

B: Yeah, it looks great.

是啊！看起來不錯耶！

深入分析

It's interesting.
有趣喔！

看見有趣的事物時，就可以主動說It's interesting，或是只要簡單地說interesting也可以，你的欣賞態度可以為你建立好的人際關係呢！

應用會話

A: Check this out.

你看！

B: It's interesting.

有趣喔！

應用會話

A: Interesting. How did you do it?

有趣喔！你是怎麼做的？

B: You really like it?

你真的喜歡嗎？

深入分析

It looks great.
看起來不錯耶！

當某件事物不錯、令你欣賞時，中文可以說「看起來不錯耶！」英文就可以說It looks great，也可以只要說looks great即可。

應用會話

A: What do you say?

你覺得如何呢？

B: It looks great.

看起來不錯耶！

應用會話

A: It looks great.

看起來不錯耶！

B: I'm glad you like it.

很高興你喜歡！

送禮給對方時，該如何知道對方是否喜歡這份禮物呢?

基礎對話

A: How do you like it?
你喜歡嗎？

B: I love it.
我喜歡！

深入分析

How do you like it?
你喜歡嗎？

想要知道對方是否喜歡某物時，就可以問How do you like it?雖然字面意思是「你如何喜歡它」，但其實就是問對方喜不喜歡的意思。

應用會話

A: How do you like it?
你喜歡嗎？

B: Oh, this one? Sure, I'm crazy about it.
喔，這個嗎？當然啊！我對這個喜歡極了！

應用會話

A: How do you like it?

你喜歡嗎？

B: Well... I don't know what to say.

這個嘛…我不知道該說什麼！

深入分析

I love it.
我喜歡！

表達喜歡某物，可以使用動詞love或like表達，最常見的句型是I love it，要注意的是it代表沒有生命的單數名稱，若是複數名稱則用them替代。

應用會話

A: What do you think of it?

你覺得如何？

B: I love it.

我喜歡！

應用會話

A: I love it.

我喜歡！

B: Me, too.

我也是！

每個人對事情的嚴重性定義未必一樣，若是產生歧見，要如何化解呢？

基礎對話

A: It happens.

常有的事。

B: It does?

真的（經常發生）嗎？

深入分析

It happens.
常有的事。

針對某事件，若對方認為不可思議、無法理解，但在你看來卻是見怪不怪，就可以說It happens，表示這是常發生的，不足為奇。

應用會話

A: It's so weird.

好奇怪！

B: It happens.

常有的事。

應用會話

A: It doesn't make sense.

沒道理啊！

B: It happens.

常有的事。

深入分析

It does?
真的嗎？

回應對方某件事的敘述，你覺得不相信，就可以反問It does?表示質疑的立場。通常是回應對方使用以it領導的一般動詞現在式說明的句子。

應用會話

A: It takes me two days to get there.

我花了兩天才到那裡！

B: It does?

真的嗎？

應用會話

A: It does?

真的這樣嗎？

B: I'm sure it does.

我確定是的！

因為對事物的見解不同，自然觀念也不相同，此時就非常適合以下的對話模式。

基礎對話

A: It's so weird.
好奇怪喔！

B: It's no big deal.
這沒什麼大不了！

深入分析

It's so weird.

好奇怪喔！

說明奇怪的形容詞很多，一般來說可以用strange表示，但是你也可以用較為嚴重、口語化的weird表達。

應用會話

A: It's so weird.
好奇怪喔！

B: I agree with what you said!
我同意你所說的。

應用會話

A: It's so weird.
好奇怪喔！

B: Yeah, it is.
是啊！的確如此！

深入分析

It's no big deal.
這沒什麼大不了！

前面提過的deal是「約定」的意思，而這裡的no big deal則是「沒什麼大不了」的意思。

應用會話

A: It's no big deal.
這沒什麼大不了！

B: Come on, you can't be serious.
拜託！你不是當真的吧？

應用會話

A: It looks terrible.
看起來很糟糕耶！

B: It's no big deal.
這沒什麼大不了！

情境 48

Track 048

人際關係是需要經營的，在路上遇到熟識的人時，該如何打招呼和回應呢？

基礎對話

A: How are you doing?
你好嗎？

B: Pretty good.
我很好！

深入分析

How are you doing?
你好嗎？

問候的方式有很多種，最常見的是How are you?而更多美國人也會使用口語化的問候語：How are you doing?

應用會話

A: How are you doing?
你好嗎？

B: I'm doing fine.
我很好！

應用會話

A: How are you doing?

你好嗎？

B: So-so.

馬馬虎虎啦！

深入分析

Pretty good.

我很好！

不管對方是真的關心或只是客套式的問候，若要回應對方的問候，你都可以說Pretty good.全文是I'm pretty good.你也可以簡單地說Fine或Good。

應用會話

A: How do you do?

你好嗎？

B: Pretty good.

我很好！

應用會話

A: How are you?

你好嗎？

B: Pretty good.

我很好！

問候的語句除了How are you doing的句子，還有其他說法嗎？若要知道對方的近況，該如何回應？

基礎對話

A: What's up?
近來好嗎？

B: I'm OK.
我很好！

深入分析

What's up?
近來好嗎？

What's up?字面意思是「什麼是向上的」，其實是關心對方近來可好的意思。

應用會話

A: What's up?
近來好嗎？

B: That's about it.
事情大概就是這樣！

應用會話

A: What's up?

近來好嗎？

B: Good enough.

非常好！

深入分析

I'm OK.

我很好！

表示自己很好的回應除了上述的I'm pretty good，當然也可以用最常見的OK表達，例如I'm OK.。

應用會話

A: You look terrible.

你看起來很糟糕！

B: I'm OK.

我很好！

應用會話

A: What's going on?

發生了什麼事？

B: Don't worry. I'm OK.

別擔心！我很好！

一個人的外表是彼此可以閒聊的話題，像是漂亮、帥氣、性感等都是不錯的讚美。

基礎對話

A: You look sexy.
你看起來很性感。

B: Are you kidding me?
你在開我玩笑吧？

深入分析

You look sexy.
你看起來很性感。

sexy不但是性感，也表示漂亮的意思，但是若你怕被對方誤會自己是否有其他的企圖，也可以只是說You look great.或You look fabulous!。look後面加形容詞。

應用會話

A: You look fabulous!
你看起來很棒啊！

B: Am I?
我是嗎？

應用會話

A: Do you like it?

你喜歡嗎？

B: Yeah. You look cute!

喜歡！你看起來好帥！

深入分析

Are you kidding me?

你在開我玩笑吧？

表示因為對方的態度或言詞不認真，所以懷疑對方是不是在開自己玩笑的意思。也可以說Are you kidding?

應用會話

A: Are you kidding me?

你在開我玩笑吧？

B: Come on, it's not so serious.

拜託，沒那麼嚴重！

應用會話

A: Are you kidding me?

你在開我玩笑吧？

B: I'm serious.

我是認真的！

除了問候對方，還想要進一步瞭解對方的生活時，該如何表達你的關心呢？

基礎對話

A: What's new?
有什麼新鮮事？

B: I got fired.
我被炒魷魚了。

深入分析

What's new?
有什麼新鮮事？

除了關心過得好不好，還可以問問對方有沒有什麼新鮮事可以分享時，就可以使用What's new?的句型。

應用會話

A: What's new?
有什麼新鮮事？

B: I had a car accident last week.
我上星期出車禍了。

應用會話

A: What's new?

有什麼新鮮事？

B: You know, still the same.

你知道的，就老樣子。

深入分析

I got fired.

我被炒魷魚了。

工作上被炒魷魚該怎麼表示？可和魷魚一點關係都沒有喔！常聽到國人說「我被fired了！」沒錯，英文的被炒魷魚叫做got fired。

應用會話

A: I got fired.

我被炒魷魚了。

B: Oh dear. I'm sorry to hear that.

哦，真是遺憾！

應用會話

A: I got fired.

我被炒魷魚了。

B: Why you?

怎麼會是你？

人際關係的經營首重相互關心，一個人的精神狀況可以從氣色表現出來，不要忘記適時的提出你的關心喔！

基礎對話

A: You look terrible.

你看起來糟透了！

B: I'm not myself today.

我今天什麼事都不對勁！

深入分析

You look terrible.
你看起來糟透了！

you look...表示「你看起來...」後面可以接形容詞，表示身體或外表的狀態，最常見的說法是you look terrible或you look great。

應用會話

A: You look terrible.

你看起來糟透了！

B: I know.

我知道啊！

應用會話

A: You look terrible.

你看起來糟透了！

B: Don't worry about me.

不要擔心我。

深入分析

I'm not myself today.

我今天什麼事都不對勁！

表示自己一整天都不順遂怎麼說？很簡單，就是「都已經不是自己」的意思，英文就是I'm not myself。

應用會話

A: You look pale. What's wrong?

你看起來臉色蒼白！怎麼啦？

B: I'm not myself today.

我今天什麼事都不對勁！

應用會話

A: You look upset. Are you OK?

你看起來心情不好！你還好嗎？

B: I'm not myself today.

我今天什麼事都不對勁！

若是對方看起來精神狀況不好，不要吝嗇付出你的關心喔！

基礎對話

A: You look upset.
你看起來很沮喪喔！

B: Don't worry about me.
不用擔心我啦！

深入分析

You look upset.
你看起來很沮喪喔！

若是對方看起來心情不好、沮喪，通常可以用upset表示。

應用會話

A: You look upset.
你看起來很沮喪喔！

B: Can I talk to you? It won't keep you long.
我能和你聊一聊嗎？不會耽誤你太久。

應用會話

A: You look upset.

你看起來很沮喪喔！

B: I have some bad news.

我有一些壞消息（要說）！

深入分析

Don't worry about me.
不用擔心我啦！

為了表示自己很好、不要讓對方擔心，面對他人的關懷，你可以說Don't worry about me。

應用會話

A: Come on, what is on your mind?

拜託！你在想什麼呢？

B: Don't worry about me.

不用擔心我啦！

應用會話

A: Don't worry about me.

不用擔心我啦！

B: But you look terrible.

但是你看起來狀況不太好！

情境 54

Track 054

寒暄關心的情境非常多，若是一方表示糟糕，而另一方並不訝異，該如何互動呢？

基礎對話

A: I was having a bad day.
我今天做什麼事都不太順利。

B: Really? Not surprised.
真的嗎？我一點都不會訝異！

深入分析

I was having a bad day.
我今天做什麼事都不太對勁。

表示自己不順遂除了可以同上述not myself表示，還可以用糟糕的一天表示：have a bad day。

應用會話

A: You look tired.
你看起來很累耶！

B: I was having a bad day.
我今天做什麼事都不太順利。

應用會話

A: I was having a bad day.

我今天做什麼事都不太順利。

B: Nothing serious, I hope.

希望不是太嚴重的事！

深入分析

Really? Not surprised.

真的？我一點都不會訝異！

當對方陳述一件讓人不訝異的事時，你就可以先反問Really?接著再說not surprised，表示並不感到意外，也就是會發生這件事是正常的。

應用會話

A: That sucks.

真糟糕！

B: Really? Not surprised.

真的嗎？我一點都不會訝異！

應用會話

A: Kenny told me so much about you.

肯尼告訴我很多有關你的事。

B: Really? Not surprised.

真的嗎？我一點都會不訝異！

人生不如意十之八九，面對失敗困境，該如何反應呢？

基礎對話

A: I didn't have a chance.
我沒有半點機會！

B: How come?
怎麼會呢？

深入分析

I didn't have a chance.
我沒有半點機會！

通常是指自己錯失機會，或無法有所為時的情境，就可以說：I didn't have a chance。

應用會話

A: I didn't have a chance.
我沒有半點機會！

B: Yeah, that is true.
是啊！那倒是事實！

應用會話

A: I didn't have a chance.

我沒有半點機會！

B: Says who?

誰說的？

深入分析

How come?

怎麼會呢？

當你想要知道原因，除了可以問why之外，另一種常見的口語化說法是How come?要注意，可不是「如何來」的意思喔！

應用會話

A: I quit.

我不想幹了！

B: How come?

怎麼會呢？

應用會話

A: Kenny couldn't come.

肯尼不能來！

B: How come?

怎麼會呢？

當彼此認知某件正在進行的事件，進度不被人瞭解時，大膽地提出是否順利執行的疑問喔！

基礎對話

A: How did it go?
事情順利吧？

B: Everything went well.
一切都順利！

深入分析

How did it go?
事情順利吧？

表示想要知道某件事目前是否順利進行時，就可以問How did it go?可不是指「如何去」的意思喔！

應用會話

A: How did it go?
事情順利吧？

B: Terrible.
糟透了！

應用會話

A: How did it go?

事情順利吧？

B: Not very well.

不太順利！

深入分析

Everything went well.

一切都順利！

回應對方對事件是否順利的關心或疑問，表示目前為止每件事都進行順利的意思。

應用會話

A: Well?

怎麼樣？

B: You see? Everything went well.

你看見了嗎！一切都順利！

應用會話

A: You look great.

你看起來氣色不錯耶！

B: Of course. Everything went well.

當然啊！一切都順利！

情境
57

Track 057

讚美是建立人際關係中不可或缺的重要因素之一，欣賞與被欣賞者之間，該如何應對呢？

基礎對話

A: You are the best.
你是最棒的。

B: Oh, I'm flattered.
喔！我受寵若驚。

深入分析

You are the best.
你是最棒的。

表示對方是雙方目前談及的某領域的佼佼者時，就可以說You are the best.。

應用會話

A: You are the best.
你是最棒的。

B: You really think so?
你真的這麼認為？

應用會話

A: You are the best.

你是最棒的。

B: Of course, I am.

我當然是啊！

深入分析

I'm flattered.
我受寵若驚。

當對方不吝嗇提出他的讚美或肯定時，中文會說「哪裡」表示客氣，而英文就可以用I'm flattered.回應。

應用會話

A: Well done, seriously.

幹得好，我是說真的！

B: I'm flattered.

我受寵若驚。

應用會話

A: Congratulations. You deserve it.

恭喜。你應得的！

B: I'm flattered.

我受寵若驚。

當男女之間發生感情時，一定都會希望能攜手一生吧！以下會話可以幫助你心想事成。

基礎對話

A: I want to spend my life with Kenny.
我想和肯尼共度一生。

B: I'm glad to hear that.
我很高興聽你這麼說。

深入分析

I want to spend my life with Kenny.
我想和肯尼共度一生。

spend someone's life with someone表示某人想和另一個人共度一輩子的意思，非常適合向對方告白時使用，例如I want to spend my life with you.

應用會話

A: I want to spend my life with Kenny.
我想和肯尼共度一生。

B: No way!
不會吧！

應用會話

A: I want to spend my life with you.

我想和你共度一生。

B: Me? Oh, no!

我？不要啊！

深入分析

I'm glad to hear that.
我很高興聽你這麼說。

glad to hear something表示高興聽聞某事，有時是真心高興，但很多時候是客套式的回應用語。

應用會話

A: We apologize for the inconvenience.

我們對於引起不便一事道歉。

B: I'm glad to hear that.

我很高興聽你這麼說。

應用會話

A: You were doing great.

你做得很棒！

B: I'm glad to hear that.

我很高興聽你這麼說。

能夠下決定是一件不簡單的事，當對方下決定要做某事或不做某事時，你該如何回應呢？

基礎對話

A: I have to stop smoking.
我必需要戒菸。

B: I'm really happy for you.
我真為你感到高興。

深入分析

I have to stop smoking.
我必需要戒菸。

stop+動名詞，表示不再做某事的意思，通常適用在戒除某種不好習慣的情境下使用，例如菸、酒等。

應用會話

A: What did the doctor say?
醫生說了些什麼？

B: I have to stop smoking.
我必需要戒菸。

應用會話

A: I have to stop drinking.

我必需要戒酒。

B: It's good for your health.

那對你的健康很好！

深入分析

I'm really happy for you.

我真為你感到高興。

表示自己很替對方感到高興時，就可以說I'm really happy for you.通常適用在對方做了某事或有某種成就時使用。

應用會話

A: She forgave me.

她原諒我了！

B: I'm really happy for you.

我真為你感到高興。

應用會話

A: I'm really happy for you.

我真為你感到高興。

B: You are?

你是嗎？

情境
60

Track 060

要守住祕密可不是一件簡單的事，例如你若中了大樂透的首獎，應該會想和他人分享，但卻又不能洩漏這個幸運，真是一種煎熬啊！

基礎對話

A: Hey, tell me your secrets.
嘿，把你的祕密告訴我吧！

B: I'm not telling.
我不會說的。

深入分析

Tell me your secrets.
把你的祕密告訴我吧！

這是一句祈使句，帶有命令口氣要求對方告知自己某事的意思。

應用會話

A: Tell me your secrets.
把你的祕密告訴我吧！

B: Why shall I?
我為什麼要告訴你？

應用會話

A: Tell me your secrets.
把你的祕密告訴我吧！
B: No way.
辦不到！

深入分析

I'm not telling.
我不會說的。

面對任何的脅迫或利誘時，自己絕對不會透露半點訊息，英文就叫做I'm not telling.

應用會話

A: Which side are you?
你要站在哪一方？
B: I'm not telling.
我不會說的。

應用會話

A: I'm not telling.
我不會說的。
B: Good. None of my business.
很好，不關我的事！

若是對方無法下決定時，該怎麼辦？你會提供自己的意見嗎？

基礎對話

A: I don't know which one is better.
我不知道哪一個比較好。

B: It's your choice.
你自己決定！

深入分析

I don't know which one is better.
我不知道哪一個比較好。

表示在兩者或一群之間無法做出選擇的意思。better是形容詞較好的，是good的比較級說法。

應用會話

A: I don't know which one is better.
我不知道哪一個比較好。

B: You are the boss.
你說了算！

應用會話

A: I don't know which one is better.
我不知道哪一個比較好。

B: I will do whatever you say!
我會依你所說的照辦！

深入分析

It's your choice.
你自己決定！

若是對方難以做出決定，你就可以說It's your choice.表示是你自己要下的決定，他人無法替你做決定。也可以說It's your own choice.表示強調的意思。

應用會話

A: I need your advice.
我需要你的建議！

B: It's your choice.
你自己決定！

應用會話

A: It's hard to make up my mind.
實在很難下決定！

B: It's your choice.
你自己決定！

情境 62

Track 062

與人言談之間，常會有一些無意思的口語用語，像是中文就有「你知道嗎...」的說法，英文該怎麼表示呢？

基礎對話

A: You know what?
你知道嗎？

B: What?
什麼？

深入分析

You know what?
你知道嗎？

當你說You know what?時，表示接下來你還有重要的事要說，希望對方能仔細聽的意思。

應用會話

A: You know what?
你知道嗎？

B: Shoot.
說吧！

應用會話

A: You know what?

你知道嗎？

B: Yeah?

什麼事？

深入分析

What?

什麼？

當你沒聽清楚對方的言詞時，就可以說What?表示自己沒聽清楚、不懂，目的是要對方解釋清楚、繼續說明或再說一次的意思。

應用會話

A: You're not gonna believe this.

你不會相信的！

B: What?

什麼？

應用會話

A: What?

什麼？

B: Never mind.

算了！

情境 63

Track 063

人際之間的相處並不是都很順遂的，當有一方對對方的行為不認同時，就可以利用以下的會話來表達。

基礎對話

A: Don't do this.
不要這麼做！

B: Why not?
為什麼不要呢？

深入分析

Don't do this.
不要這麼做！

直接說明希望對方不要做某事的警告用語，this表示對方正在從事的這個行為。

應用會話

A: Don't do this.
不要這麼做！

B: I have to.
我必須這麼做！

應用會話

A: Don't do this.

不要這麼做！

B: It's none of your business!

你少管閒事！

深入分析

Why not?

為什麼不要呢？

當對方陳述某件否定語句時，若你不認同，就可以反問對方Why not?，表示希望對方給個理由說明不要的原因。

應用會話

A: I don't need it.

我用不著了。

B: Why not?

為什麼不要呢？

應用會話

A: Why not?

為什麼不要呢？

B: No reason.

就沒有理由啊！

情境 64

Track 064

若是有一方遭受不被相信的對待，應該要如何回應呢？不要吝嗇付出你的關心喔！

基礎對話

A: They don't believe you, do they?
他們不相信你，對吧？

B: How do you know?
你怎麼會知道？

深入分析

They don't believe you, do they?
他們不相信你，對吧？

可能是對方不被某些人相信，而你藉由這句問句來關心、確認的意思。

應用會話

A: They don't believe you, do they?
他們不相信你，對吧？

B: No, they don't.
不，他們不相信！

應用會話

A: They don't believe you, do they?

他們不相信你，對吧？

B: Maybe.

也許是吧！

深入分析

How do you know?

你怎麼會知道？

當你認為不會有人知道某事，偏偏對方就是知道時，你就可以訝異地追問對方How do you know?，表示自己不敢相信的意思。

應用會話

A: How do you know?

你怎麼會知道？

B: You tell me.

你說呢？

應用會話

A: How do you know?

你怎麼會知道？

B: I do not know.

我不知道啊！

世事難料，當發生令人感到不可思議的事件時，要如何應對呢？

基礎對話

A: I can't believe it.
我真不敢相信！

B: Easy!
放輕鬆點！

深入分析

I can't believe it.
我真不敢相信！

當某事發生，實在令人難以置信、不可思議時，你就可以說I can't believe it.，也可以簡單的說Unbelievable!表示難以相信的意思。

應用會話

A: I can't believe it.
我真不敢相信！

B: It is true.
是真的！

應用會話

A: I can't believe it.

我真不敢相信！

B: No wonder.

一點都不奇怪！

深入分析

Easy!

放輕鬆點！

當對方情緒緊張、失控時，你唯一要做的就是安撫對方，此時就可以拍拍對方的肩膀說Easy，讓對方不要緊張、放輕鬆的意思。

應用會話

A: Easy!

放輕鬆點！

B: I just can't.

我辦不到啊！

應用會話

A: What? What did you just say?

什麼？你說什麼？

B: Easy!

放輕鬆點！

情境 66

Track 066

情緒波動難免會需要抒發的時候，面對這樣的狀況，恐怕先離開現場會好一些。

基礎對話

A: I need some fresh air.
我要呼吸一點新鮮空氣！

B: OK. Let's go for a ride.
好啊！我們開車去逛逛吧！

深入分析

I need some fresh air.
我要呼吸一點新鮮空氣！

通常表示要離開現場，所以用「要呼吸新鮮空氣」當藉口離席的意思。當然也可以是真的覺得悶，想要呼吸新鮮空氣的意思。

應用會話

A: You look upset. Are you OK?
你看起來很沮喪！你還好嗎？

B: I need some fresh air.
我要呼吸一點新鮮空氣！

應用會話

A: I need some fresh air.

我要呼吸一點新鮮空氣！

B: What happened to you?

你怎麼啦？

深入分析

Let's go for a ride.

我們開車去逛逛吧！

ride是指車程，而go for a ride則是開車出去閒逛的意思。

應用會話

A: Let's go for a ride.

我們開車去逛逛吧！

B: Sure, why not?

好啊！

應用會話

A: Let's go for a ride.

我們開車去逛逛吧！

B: Oh, I don't think so.

喔，不好吧！

俗諺「言者無心、聽者有意」，別因為口語之間不同見解，而讓彼此產生的誤會。

基礎對話

A: You know what I mean?

你知道我的意思嗎？

B: Got it.

我知道！

深入分析

You know what I mean?

你知道我的意思嗎？

為了要確認對方瞭不瞭解自己的原意，不要忘記和對方確認一下喔！

應用會話

A: You know what I mean?

你知道我的意思嗎？

B: Go ahead.

你說啊！

應用會話

A: You know what I mean?

你知道我的意思嗎？

B: You mean...

你的意思是…

深入分析

Got it.

我知道！

got it的字面是「得到它」，其實就是表示「瞭解」、「我懂」的意思，是非常口語化的用法，通常適用在回應對方自己已經瞭解的情境。

應用會話

A: Let me know if you need any other help.

如果你需要其他幫助，讓我知道一下！

B: Got it.

我知道！

應用會話

A: Just do what I said.

照我說的去做！

B: Got it.

我知道！

情境
68

Track 068

當你想要知道某人是否做了某事，如何詢問呢？

基礎對話

A: Did you get what you want?
你有拿到想要的東西了嗎？

B: Yes, I did.
有，我有！

深入分析

Did you get what you want?

你有拿到想要的東西了嗎？

詢問對方是否做某事時，通常可以使用過去式Did you...的問句。what you want是指「你想要的東西」，而不是「什麼是你想要」的意思。

應用會話

A: Did you get what you want?
你有拿到想要的東西了嗎？

B: No, I did not.
沒有，我沒有！

應用會話

A: Did you get what you want?

你有拿到想要的東西了嗎？

B: Not really.

不盡然！

深入分析

Yes, I did.

有，我有！

通常是肯定句回應對方以過去式did you...為主的問句，例如對方問Did you have your dinner?時，你就可以回應Yes, I did.或是否定的No, I didn't.（不，我沒有）。

應用會話

A: Did you go to see a doctor?

你有去看醫生了嗎？

B: Yes, I did.

有，我有！

應用會話

A: Did you check your e-mail?

你有收信了嗎？

B: Yes, I did.

有，我有！

情境 69

Track 069

分享是人際間表示友善的一種態度，朋友之間就是需要這樣的互動，才能建立良好的人際關係。

基礎對話

A: Check this out!

你看！

B: I see nothing.

我沒有看到有東西啊！

深入分析

Check this out!

你看！

非常口語化的用法，表示你過來看看 (check) 這個東西的意思，可和退房 (check out) 無關喔！

應用會話

A: Check this out!

你看！

B: Wow, cool!

哇！真酷！

應用會話

A: Check this out!

你看！

B: They look great.

他們看起來不錯耶！

深入分析

I see nothing.

我沒有看到有東西啊！

see nothing字面意思是「看到沒事」，但其實是表示「沒有看到任何東西」的意思。

應用會話

A: I see nothing.

我沒有看到有東西啊！

B: Are you kidding me?

你是開玩笑的吧？

應用會話

A: What do you think of it?

你覺得怎麼樣？

B: What? I see nothing.

什麼東西？我沒有看到有東西啊！

感情的經營是需要跨出第一步的，偶爾也要關心一下未婚的朋友的感情生活喔！

基礎對話

A: How was your date?
你的約會怎麼樣了？

B: He stood me up again.
他又放我鴿子了。

深入分析

How was your date?
你的約會怎麼樣了？

通常表示你知道對方之前曾經有約會的對象，也想要知道他們兩人約會的結果如何的意思。

應用會話

A: How was your date?
你的約會怎麼樣了？

B: Sucks.
糟透了！

應用會話

A: How was your date?

你的約會怎麼樣了？

B: He's cute and mature.

他很帥，也很成熟。

深入分析

He stood me up again.

他又放我鴿子了。

若是對方沒有依約出現，就是中文的「放鴿子」，英文可和鴿子一點關係都沒有，而是stood someone up的句型。

應用會話

A: He stood me up again.

他又放我鴿子了。

B: Oh, poor girl.

喔，可憐的女孩！

應用會話

A: He stood me up again.

他又放我鴿子了。

B: He what?

他幹了什麼好事？

針對某件事物的好與壞，若想要聽聽對方的意見，就可以適用以下的情境會話喔！

基礎對話

A: Is it good enough?
夠好嗎？

B: Not even close.
差太遠了！

深入分析

Is it good enough?
夠好嗎？

中文常說的「夠不夠好？」是指某事物好的程度有多少，英文就叫做Is it good enough?，也可以簡單地說Good enough?。

應用會話

A: Is it good enough?
夠好嗎？

B: It looks great.
看起來不錯！

應用會話

A: Is it good enough?

夠好嗎？

B: Not as good as I thought.

沒有我想像中的這麼好！

深入分析

Not even close.

差太遠了！

回應對方的猜測，表示結果和對方的認知差很多，有點類似中文「連邊都談不上」的意思。

應用會話

A: Not even close.

差太遠了！

B: Oh. That bad?

喔？有這麼糟？

應用會話

A: Not even close.

差太遠了！

B: How come?

為什麼？

情境 72

Track 072

想要知道對方的意見的說法有許多種，以下是就外表的視覺來決定好與壞的情境。

基礎對話

A: Does it really look OK?

看起來還真的不錯嗎？

B: Yeah, I think so.

是啊！我認為是如此。

深入分析

Does it really look OK?

看起來還真的不錯嗎？

表示某事物的外觀或就視覺上來判斷，是否不錯或合乎期待的意思。

應用會話

A: Does it really look OK?

看起來還真的不錯嗎？

B: Why not?

就是啊！

應用會話

A: Does it really look OK?

看起來還真的不錯嗎？

B: Yes, it does.

是啊！

深入分析

Yeah, I think so.
是啊！我認為是如此。

對方可能已經陳述某一觀念，你不但同意，也認為是如此的狀況時，就可以說Yeah, I think so.，有時也代表答應的情境。

應用會話

A: Can you save my place, please?

你能幫我保留位子嗎？

B: Yeah, I think so.

是啊！我認為是如此。

應用會話

A: Maybe you can lease a car.

也許你可以貸款買車。

B: Yeah, I think so.

是啊！我認為是如此。

搭訕是人際關係建立的第一步，如何和第一次見面的陌生人打開話匣子呢？

基礎對話

A: By the way, I'm Kenny.
對了，我是肯尼。

B: I've heard so much about you.
久仰大名！

深入分析

By the way, I'm Kenny.
對了，我是肯尼。

可能已經先和對方聊了一兩句後，才介紹自己的名字。By the way,...類似中文的「對了，...」表示後面還有要說明的事。

應用會話

A: By the way, I'm Kenny.
對了，我是肯尼。

B: My pleasure to meet you.
很高興認識你！

應用會話

A: By the way, my name is Kenny.

對了，我是肯尼。

B: I am Jessica.

我是潔西卡。

深入分析

I've heard so much about you.

久仰大名！

通常是對方先自我介紹身份後，你才表示自己聽過對方的名號，就可以說I've heard so much about you.，類似中文的「久仰大名」。

應用會話

A: I've heard so much about you.

久仰大名！

B: Hope nothing bad.

希望不是壞事！

應用會話

A: Hi, I am Kenny, Tina's father.

嗨，我是肯尼，是蒂娜的父親！

B: I've heard so much about you.

久仰大名！

朋友之間閒聊難免會提及自己以前的風光事蹟，如果太誇張，你會相信嗎？

基礎對話

A: I used to be a singer.
我以前曾經是歌手。

B: Is that a joke?
這是開玩笑嗎？

深入分析

I used to be a singer.
我以前曾經是歌手。

used to…表示「過去曾經...」，通常是說明過去的某個經歷或身份，to的後面可以加be或一般動詞。

應用會話

A: I used to be a singer.
我以前曾經是歌手。

B: I can't believe it.
真教人不敢相信！

應用會話

A: They used to go swimming.

他們過去常常去游泳。

B: What happened now?

後來發生什麼事？

深入分析

Is that a joke?

這是開玩笑嗎？

對於對方的言論感到不相信，不但懷疑，甚至覺得對方是開玩笑的。

應用會話

A: Is that a joke?

這是開玩笑嗎？

B: No. I'm serious.

不是！我是認真的！

應用會話

A: Is that a joke?

這是開玩笑嗎？

B: Sorry. I didn't mean to.

抱歉！我不是故意的。

購買衣物時，一般人都會提出的問題就是試穿的需求，千萬不要放棄試穿的權利喔！

基礎對話

A: Can I try it on?
我可以試穿嗎？

B: No problem.
可以啊！

深入分析

Can I try it on?

我可以試穿嗎？

try on是試穿衣物的意思，一般來說，只要不是特價商品，店家都應該有提供試穿的服務，但還是禮貌性詢問確認較佳。

應用會話

A: Can I try it on?
我可以試穿嗎？

B: Sure, go ahead.
當然可以！

應用會話

A: Can I try it on?

我可以試穿嗎？

B: I'm afraid not.

恐怕不可以！

深入分析

No problem.

可以啊！

當對方提出某個要求時，若你答應，就可以豪氣地回應No problem.表示「沒問題、好啊！」的樂意態度。No problem.也表示對道謝者的「不客氣」回應。

應用會話

A: Can I open the window?

我能打開窗戶嗎？

B: No problem.

可以啊！

應用會話

A: Thank you so much.

謝謝你！

B: No problem.

不必客氣！

送禮的時候該怎麼說呢？面對要送禮物給對方或接受禮物的情境，簡單的一句話就可以表達喔！

基礎對話

A: I have something for you.

我有東西要給你！

B: It's for me?

是要給我的？

深入分析

I have something for you.
我有東西要給你！

have something for someone表示有東西要給某人，既可以是送禮的意思，也可以只是拿取物品給某人的意思。

應用會話

A: I have something for you.

我有東西要給你！

B: Wow! I love it.

哇，我好喜歡啊！

應用會話

A: I have something for you.

我有東西要給你！

B: Whatever it is, I'm going to return it.

管他是什麼，我要去退還！

深入分析

It's for me?

是要給我的？

當你收到對方給你的禮物時，可以訝異地表示「給我的嗎？」英文就叫做It's for me?

應用會話

A: Surprise! Here you are.

給你一個驚喜！給你！

B: It's for me?

是要給我的？

應用會話

A: It's for me?

是要給我的？

B: Sure. You look forward to it, don't you?

當然！你很期待這個，不是嗎？

人際之間的互動關係中，提供建議是很正常的，面對建議被採納，你該如何回應？

基礎對話

A: I took your advice.
我有聽你的建議！

B: Good for you.
對你來說是好的！

深入分析

I took your advice.

我有聽你的建議！

took someone's advice字面意思是拿某人的建議，也就是聽從、採納某人的建議的意思。

應用會話

A: I took your advice.
我有聽你的建議！

B: Then what happened?
然後發生什麼事了？

應用會話

A: I took your advice.

我有聽你的建議！

B: You did?

你有嗎？

深入分析

Good for you.

對你來說是好的！

當得知對方的某事或某決定時，若這件事是對對方有好處的，就可以回應Good for you，全文的說法是It's good for you.。若是不好的事，則是Bad for you.。

應用會話

A: I don't want to think about it.

我盡量不去想這件事。

B: Good for you.

對你來說是好的！

應用會話

A: We're not seeing each other anymore.

我們已經沒有在一起了。

B: Good for you.

對你來說是好的！

若要人不知，除非己莫為，當事情紙包不住火時，就大方承認吧！

基礎對話

A: How do you know so much?
你怎麼會知道這麼多事？

B: It's a secret.
這是祕密！

深入分析

How do you know so much?
你怎麼會知道這麼多事？

通常在對方知道了一些本來不被人所知的事，或是對方上知天文下知地理時，就可以好奇地詢問對方：How do you know so much?

應用會話

A: How do you know so much?
你怎麼會知道這麼多事？

B: I just know it.
我就是知道。

應用會話

A: That's all about it.

事情就是這樣！

B: How do you know so much?

你怎麼會知道這麼多事？

深入分析

It's a secret.

這是祕密！

表示目前這件事是個祕密，所以自己不會再透露更多相關細節，也可以讓對方知難而退的意思。

應用會話

A: When will it be ready?

什麼時候能準備好？

B: It's a secret.

這是祕密！

應用會話

A: It's a secret.

這是祕密！

B: So you're not gonna tell me?

所以你不打算告訴我囉？

在路上遇到可能熟識的人時，彼此該如何應對呢？

基礎對話

A: Your name is Kenny, right?
你是肯尼對吧？

B: Yes, I am.
是的，我就是！

深入分析

Your name is Kenny, right?
你是肯尼對吧？

表示猜測對方的身份，但自己不是很確認的問句，也可以用 " You must be someone " 的句型來確定對方的身份。

應用會話

A: Your name is Kenny, right?
你是肯尼對吧？

B: No, I am not.
不，我不是！

應用會話

A: Your name is Kenny, right?

你是肯尼對吧？

B: Do I know you?

我們認識嗎？

深入分析

Yes, I am.

是的，我就是！

例如對方提出某個以be動詞為主的問句，若你的回應是肯定的，就可以回應Yes, I am.，若是否定，則為No, I am not.。

應用會話

A: Are you busy now?

你現在忙嗎？

B: Yes, I am.

是的，我就是！

應用會話

A: Are you in a hurry?

你有急事嗎？

B: No, I am not.

沒有，我不會啊！

情境 80

Track 080

關於好或不好的答案只能用yes或no嗎？I don't think so.（我不這麼認為），你可以回應的方式有很多種啊！

基礎對話

A: Can I have a look?

我可以看一下嗎？

B: I don't think so.

我不這麼認為。

深入分析

Can I have a look?

我可以看一下嗎？

想要一探究竟或看一眼的要求時，可以用have a look的句型。

應用會話

A: Can I have a look?

我可以看一下嗎？

B: Go ahead.

可以！

應用會話

A: Can I have a look?

我可以看一下嗎？

B: Why? What do you want to know?

為什麼？你想知道什麼？

深入分析

I don't think so.

我不這麼認為。

I don't think so.字面意思雖然是「我不這麼認為」，但也可以適用在否定的回答情境中，相對的，若是肯定的回應，則可以說I think so.。

應用會話

A: Can you help me with this?

可以幫我這個忙嗎？

B: I don't think so.

我不這麼認為。

應用會話

A: Maybe that will help.

也許會有幫助。

B: Yeah, I think so.

是啊，我是這麼認為的！

Track 081

男女之間的關係可不是一個人說了就算的，想要安定的一方遇到還想尋尋覓覓的一方，該怎麼辦呢？

基礎對話

A: I don't want to go steady.
我不想定下來。

B: I couldn't agree less.
我是絕對不會同意的。

深入分析

I don't want to go steady.
我不想定下來。

go steady可不是「去安定」，而是尋求穩定關係的立場，適用在男女關係的相處上。

應用會話

A: I don't want to go steady.
我不想定下來。

B: How come?
為什麼？

應用會話

A: I don't want to go steady.

我不想定下來。

B: Neither do I.

我也不要！

深入分析

I couldn't agree less.

我是絕對不會同意的。

字面意思是「無法再少同意」，也就是「絕對不同意」的意思。

應用會話

A: What do you say?

你覺得如何呢？

B: I couldn't agree less.

我是絕對不會同意的。

應用會話

A: I couldn't agree less.

我是絕對不會同意的。

B: Give me a break. I wasn't born yesterday.

少來了！我又不是三歲小孩！

情境 82

Track 082

人與人之間難免會因為意見不和而有爭執，該如何說明爭執的情境呢？

基礎對話

A: Did you have a fight?
你們吵架啦？

B: Not really.
不盡然！

深入分析

Did you have a fight?

你們吵架啦？

have a fight除了可以是打架之外，也可以是口語上爭吵、吵架的意思。

應用會話

A: Did you have a fight?
你們吵架啦？

B: How do you know?
你怎麼會知道？

應用會話

A: Did you have a fight?

你們吵架啦？

B: Yeap!

是啊！

深入分析

Not really.

不盡然！

對於對方的說明你不完全認同時，就可以如此回應，表示事實非如對方所言。

應用會話

A: Don't you think she's a nice girl?

你不覺得她是好女孩嗎？

B: Not really.

不盡然！

應用會話

A: Not really.

不盡然！

B: Why not?

為什麼不是？

當男女之間產生愛的火花時，常會深陷其中，如何詮釋男女雙方的感情生活呢？

基礎對話

A: They fall in love.
他們兩人陷入熱戀了！

B: No shit!
不會吧！

深入分析

They fall in love.
他們兩人陷入熱戀了！

和字面意思一樣，fall in love就是「陷入熱戀」，表示雙方正在談戀愛的熱戀期中。

應用會話

A: They fall in love.
他們兩人陷入熱戀了！

B: It can't be.
不可能的事吧！

應用會話

A: They fall in love.

他們兩人陷入熱戀了！

B: Since when?

從什麼時候開始的？

深入分析

No shit!

不會吧！

表示對所聽到的是感到不可思議或不敢相信的意思，因為是非正式語言，要特別注意使用的時機。

應用會話

A: Be here on time at six sharp tomorrow.

明天六點鐘準時過來！

B: No shit! So early?

不會吧！這麼早？

應用會話

A: No shit!

不會吧！

B: I beg your pardon!

你說什麼？

對事情感到不可思議的說法有許多種，以下的情境也適合說明這個令人難以相信的事件。

基礎對話

A: It doesn't make any sense.
沒有道理啊！

B: Nobody cares!
沒人會在乎！

深入分析

It doesn't make any sense.
沒有道理啊！

表示對所聽聞的事件覺得沒有道理、難以令人信服。make sense是「有道理」的意思。

應用會話

A: It doesn't make any sense.
沒有道理啊！

B: It's none of your business!
你少管閒事！

應用會話

A: It doesn't make any sense.

沒有道理啊！

B: I have no choice.

我別無選擇啊！

深入分析

Nobody cares!

沒人會在乎！

care是指在意、關心，Nobody cares!表示強調沒有人會在意或關注的意思。

應用會話

A: Nobody cares!

沒人會在乎！

B: Poor girl.

可憐的女孩！

應用會話

A: Nobody cares!

沒人會在乎！

B: But I do.

但是我會（在意）啊！

要和朋友分享新鮮物要如何表示？可以請對方先瞧一瞧啊！

基礎對話

A: Look what I've got.

你看我有什麼東西！

B: Where did you get this?

你從哪裡得到這個的？

深入分析

Look what I've got.
你看我有什麼東西！

表示要對方來看看自己目前手上所擁有的物品，look what...表示「所要看的東西」的意思。

應用會話

A: Look what I've got.

你看我有什麼東西！

B: It's awesome.

真酷！

應用會話

A: Look what I've got.
你看我有什麼東西！

B: I've never seen it before.
我以前從沒有看過這個東西！

深入分析

Where did you get this?
你從哪裡得到這個的？

表示對於對方的東西感到好奇，想要知道擁有的來源的意思。

應用會話

A: Where did you get it?
你從哪裡得到這個的？

B: My father bought it for me.
我父親送我的！

應用會話

A: Where did you get it?
你從哪裡得到這個的？

B: I'm not gonna tell you.
我不告訴你！

認同對方的意見就該讓對方知道，認同的態度該如何表示呢？

基礎對話

A: I bet it cost a fortune?
我猜這個很貴喔？

B: I will say.
的確是這樣。

深入分析

I bet it cost a fortune?
我猜這個很貴喔？

cost a fortune表示價值不斐的意思。而I bet...類似中文「我賭一定是...」，帶有「肯定是...」的意思。

應用會話

A: I bet it cost a fortune?
我猜這個很貴喔？

B: No, not at all.
不，一點都不會！

應用會話

A: Check this out.

你看！

B: I bet it cost a fortune?

我猜這個很貴喔？

深入分析

I will say.

的確是這樣。

字面意思是「我會說」，其實是認同對方的言論，表示我也會這麼說或這麼認為的意思。

應用會話

A: He's under a lot of pressure, right?

他的壓力很大，對吧？

B: I will say.

的確是這樣。

應用會話

A: Can it happen again?

事情會再發生嗎？

B: I will say.

的確是這樣。

情境 87

Track 087

下結論和認同對方意見，其實只要簡單兩三個單字就能表達。

基礎對話

A: What a bargain!
真是划算啊！

B: I know.
我知道啊！

深入分析

What a bargain!
真是划算啊！

What...可不是疑問句，而是表示「真是...」的意思。

應用會話

A: What a bargain!
真是划算啊！

B: So you want to buy it?
所以你想要買囉？

應用會話

A: See? It costs 10 dollars.

看吧！只要價十元。

B: What a bargain!

真是划算啊！

深入分析

I know.
我知道啊！

表示對方所說的是自己已經了然於胸，不用對方再解釋的意思。

應用會話

A: They broke up last month.

他們上個月分手了！

B: I know.

我知道啊！

應用會話

A: You have to be there on time.

你得要準時抵達那裡。

B: I know.

我知道啊！

情境
88

Track 088

面對抱怨的聲音，該如何自處呢？「致歉」是第一要件喔！

基礎對話

A: What a mess over here.
這裡真是一團亂！

B: I'm terribly sorry.
我真的很抱歉！

深入分析

What a mess over here.
這裡真是一團亂！

mess是指混亂，What a mess.表示真的很亂的意思。

應用會話

A: What a mess over here.
這裡真是一團亂！

B: It's Kenny's fault.
是肯尼的錯！

應用會話

A: What a mess over here.

這裡真是一團亂！

B: I did nothing.

我什麼事都沒做啊！

深入分析

I'm terribly sorry.

我真的很抱歉！

道歉也分等級，一般的道歉只要說I'm sorry.或是Sorry!，若是「非常抱歉」則可以說I'm terribly sorry.，terribly是非常地的意思。

應用會話

A: I'm terribly sorry.

我真的很抱歉！

B: Never mind.

沒關係！

應用會話

A: I'm terribly sorry.

我真的很抱歉！

B: You should be.

你是要感到抱歉！

你是個健忘或記性好的人？要常常運用大腦的記憶功能，才不會老是忘東忘西的！

基礎對話

A: Do you remember that?

你記得嗎？

B: I don't remember.

我不記得耶！

深入分析

Do you remember that?
你記得嗎？

Do you remember...表示詢問對方是否記得某事、某物或某人的意思。that可以用任何名詞替代。

應用會話

A: Do you remember Kenny's address?

你記得肯尼的地址嗎？

B: No, I don't.

不，我不記得！

應用會話

A: Do you remember Penny?

你記得潘妮嗎？

B: Yes, I do. This name rings a bell.

我記得！這名字好熟！

深入分析

I don't remember.

我不記得耶！

若是不記得某事，就可以直接說I don't remember.。

應用會話

A: I don't remember.

我不記得耶！

B: How come? He is your friend, isn't he?

怎麼會呢？他是你的朋友，不是嗎？

應用會話

A: I don't remember.

我不記得耶！

B: Good relief.

幸好！

現代的人生活緊湊，若是需要花很多時間去做的事，很多人往往會因為騰不出時間而拒絕，此時該如何應對呢？

基礎對話

A: It'll only take you 5 minutes.
只會花你五分鐘的時間。

B: Good. This will save me a lot of time.
很好！這樣會節省我很多時間。

深入分析

It'll only take you 5 minutes.
只會花你五分鐘的時間。

時間的花費通常用spend或take這兩個單字，" take someone+時間 " 表示花費某人某段時間的意思。

應用會話

A: How long will it be?
會需要多久的時間？

B: It'll only take you 5 minutes.
只會花你五分鐘的時間。

應用會話

A: It'll only take us 5 minutes.

只會花我們五分鐘的時間。

B: OK. It's fine with me.

好，我可以！

深入分析

This will save me a lot of time.
這樣會節省我很多時間。

節省時間則是用save這個單字，常用片語是＂save someone＋時間＂。someone通常是受詞him、her、us、them或人名。

應用會話

A: This will save me a lot of time.

這樣會節省我很多時間。

B: OK, let's go.

好，我們走吧！

應用會話

A: This will save me a lot of time.

這樣會節省我很多時間。

B: So you are in?

所以你要參加囉？

在路上遇見熟人該如何表示呢？不要忘記要和對方多多閒聊、寒暄喔！

基礎對話

A: So glad we bumped into each other!

真高興遇到你！

B: What a small world.

世界真的很小！

深入分析

So glad we bumped into each other!
真高興遇到你！

bump into表示偶遇的意思。So glad...的全文是I'm so glad...，表示「我很高興...」。

應用會話

A: So glad we bumped into each other!

真高興遇到你！

B: Me, too.

我也很高興！

應用會話

A: So glad we bumped into each other!

真高興遇到你！

B: Give me a call if you have a chance.

有機會的話要打電話給我。

深入分析

What a small world.

世界真的很小！

和字面意思一樣，世界真是小，通常適用在碰巧發生某事或和某人偶遇的場合。

應用會話

A: Kenny? What are you doing here?

肯尼嗎？你在這裡幹嘛？

B: Hi, what a small world.

嗨，世界真的很小！

應用會話

A: I ran into my ex-wife.

我遇到了我的前妻。

B: What a small world.

世界真的很小！

想要聊一聊八卦嗎？希望對方多透露一點消息嗎？不妨多多利用以下的對話。

基礎對話

A: Tell me more.
再多告訴我一點。

B: About what?
有關什麼事？

深入分析

Tell me more.
再多告訴我一點。

希望對方告訴自己某事時，就可以直接說Tell me more.表示自己很想再多知道一點有關兩人正在談論的這件事的意思。

應用會話

A: Tell me more.
再多告訴我一點。

B: I don't know the answer. You tell me.
我不知道答案！你告訴我啊！

應用會話

A: Tell me more.

再多告訴我一點。

B: No, not now, please.

不要，拜託不要現在。

深入分析

About what?
有關什麼事？

不懂對方指的是何事時，就可以簡短地問About what?，表示自己不清楚是關於何事的意思。

應用會話

A: About what?

有關什麼事？

B: About our unborn child.

是有關我們還未出世的孩子！

應用會話

A: I'm sorry about that.

我為此感到抱歉。

B: About what?

有關什麼事？

情境
93

Track 093

和人閒聊時，常會有一些口語沒有太多意義的用語，此時就適合以下的對話情境。

基礎對話

A: I'll tell you what...
你知道嗎？

B: I'm listening.
我在聽！

深入分析

I'll tell you what...
你知道嗎？

字面意思是「我會告訴你...」，其實和中文的「你知道嗎？」通常後面有更重要的事要說明，而希望對方仔細聽的意思。

應用會話

A: I'll tell you what...
你知道嗎？

B: Sorry, I have no time now.
抱歉，我現在沒有時間。

應用會話

A: I'll tell you what...

你知道嗎？

B: Yes?

什麼？

深入分析

I'm listening.

我在聽！

字面意思是「我正在聽！」也就是鼓勵對方繼續說下去，類似中文「我洗耳恭聽」的意思。

應用會話

A: Are you there?

你有在聽嗎？

B: I'm listening.

我在聽！

應用會話

A: I'm listening.

我在聽！

B: I might get a job one day soon.

我很快就會找到工作。

人多嘴雜，若是大家的認知或看法不同，要如何面對這個不同調的狀況呢？

基礎對話

A: That doesn't sound too bad.
聽起來不會太糟糕啊！

B: Not funny.
不有趣喔！

深入分析

That doesn't sound too bad.
聽起來不會太糟糕啊！

表示某件事就你的立場來說，聽起來似乎不會太糟糕的意思。

應用會話

A: That doesn't sound too bad.
聽起來不會太糟糕啊！

B: Are you kidding me?
你是開玩笑的吧？

應用會話

A: That doesn't sound too bad.

聽起來不會太糟糕啊！

B: What? It's terrible.

什麼呀！很糟糕！

深入分析

Not funny.
不有趣喔！

通常是對方在耍幽默，而在你看來，一點幽默感都沒有，也不認同對方的意思。

應用會話

A: Oh, I don't think you want to know.

喔，我不認為你會想要知道！

B: Not funny.

不有趣喔！

應用會話

A: Not funny.

不有趣喔！

B: I know how you feel.

我知道你的感受！

面對自我感覺良好的人，恐怕許多人都會不認同吧！

基礎對話

A: Don't flatter yourself !
別往你自己臉上貼金。

B: Come on, it's just a joke.
拜託，開玩笑的啦！

深入分析

Don't flatter yourself!
別往你自己臉上貼金。

表示要對方清醒些，不要再自我感覺良好。

應用會話

A: Don't flatter yourself !
別往你自己臉上貼金。

B: But I'm serious.
但是我是認真的！

應用會話

A: See? It's really something.

看吧？很了不起吧！

B: Don't flatter yourself!

別往你自己臉上貼金。

深入分析

Come on, it's just a joke.

拜託，開玩笑的啦！

表示要對方不要這麼嚴肅，一切都是開玩笑的！

應用會話

A: Hey, it can't be true.

嘿，不可能是真的吧！

B: Come on, it's just a joke.

拜託，開玩笑的啦！

應用會話

A: Come on, it's just a joke.

拜託，開玩笑的啦！

B: Not funny.

不有趣喔！

一個人是玩笑態度，另一個則是認真的，不同調的兩人要如何相處呢？

基礎對話

A: Are you kidding me?

你是開玩笑的吧？

B: I'm serious.

我是認真的。

深入分析

Are you kidding me?

你是開玩笑的吧？

詢問對方是不是開自己玩笑的意思，也表示自己不認同對方的言論，所以反問的意思。

應用會話

A: Did you know that he married Penny?

你知道他和潘妮結婚了嗎？

B: Are you kidding me?

你是開玩笑的吧？

應用會話

A: Did you know he was having an affair?

你知道他有外遇了嗎？

B: Are you kidding me?

你是開玩笑的吧？

深入分析

I'm serious.
我是認真的。

表示自己是認真的、不是開玩笑的立場，並希望對方也能嚴肅看待。

應用會話

A: I'm serious.

我是認真的。

B: Me, too.

我也是。

應用會話

A: I'm serious.

我是認真的。

B: Knock it off.

你少來這一套！

情境
97

Track 097

立場不同的表達方式有許多種，以下則是間接地詢問對方是否所言是玩笑話的意思。

基礎對話

A: You can't be serious.
你不是當真的吧？

B: I meant it.
我是認真的。

深入分析

You can't be serious.

你不是當真的吧？

表示對於對方的立場感到懷疑，並認為對方不是認真的態度。

應用會話

A: You can't be serious.
你不是當真的吧？

B: I'm not kidding.
我不是開玩笑的。

應用會話

A: You can't be serious.

你不是當真的吧？

B: What do you say?

你說呢？

深入分析

I meant it.
我是認真的。

字面意思是「我就是這個意思」，也就是「我所言是真的」的意思。

應用會話

A: I meant it.

我是認真的。

B: Oh, this is great.

喔，很好啊！

深入分析

A: I meant it.

我是認真的。

B: I can't believe it.

我真不敢相信！

事情的發展往往令人感到訝異，面對這種變化，很多人都難以接受吧！

基礎對話

A: You must be kidding.
你是在開玩笑的吧！

B: You never know.
世事難料喔！

深入分析

You must be kidding.
你是在開玩笑的吧！

表示你認為對方一定是開玩笑的，自己並為此感到不可思議的意思。

應用會話

A: You must be kidding.
你是在開玩笑的吧！

B: It's the truth.
這就是事實！

應用會話

A: It's time for us to say " No " to Kenny.

該是我們對肯尼說不的時候了。

B: You must be kidding.

你是在開玩笑的吧！

深入分析

You never know.
世事難料喔！

字面意思是「你永遠不知道」，也就是世事難料，後續發展很難被事先預知的意思。

應用會話

A: You never know.

世事難料喔！

B: It sounds like you accepted it.

聽起來你接受它了！

應用會話

A: They won't do this to us.

他們不會這麼對我們。

B: You never know.

世事難料喔！

情境 99

詢問是否開玩笑的說法有許多種，該如何說明自己不確定的立場？

基礎對話

A: No kidding?

不是開玩笑的吧！

B: I'm not really sure.

我不太清楚！

深入分析

No kidding?

不是開玩笑的吧！

用詢問語氣問「不是開玩笑的吧？」也就是表示自己不相信對方是認真的意思。

應用會話

A: I don't want to see him anymore!

我不願再見到他！

B: No kidding?

不是開玩笑的吧！

應用會話

A: He's the richest person in the world.

他是世界上最有錢的人。

B: No kidding?

不是開玩笑的吧！

深入分析

I'm not really sure.

我不太清楚！

表示自己也不清楚狀況的意思，所以很難明確告訴對方。

應用會話

A: Do you where he is?

你知道他在哪裡嗎？

B: I'm not really sure.

我不太清楚！

應用會話

A: Things cannot go worse than that at the worst.

事情不會比這更糟吧？

B: I'm not really sure.

我不太清楚！

對於不確定的事產生懷疑，你有權利要弄清楚，千萬不要莫名其妙接受喔！

基礎對話

A: Are you sure?
你確定？

B: There is no doubt about it.
那是毫無疑問的。

深入分析

Are you sure?
你確定？

希望對方能明確告知自己，他/她的立場是否肯定或確定的意思。也可以說Are you sure about it?。

應用會話

A: Are you sure?
你確定？

B: I have nothing to do with it.
那與我無關。

應用會話

A: Are you sure about it?

對那件事你有確定嗎？

B: That's for sure.

那是肯定的。

深入分析

There is no doubt about it.

那是毫無疑問的。

表示自己的肯定立場，對於某事（it）是不容懷疑的。

應用會話

A: Kenny never tells the truth.

肯尼從來就不會說實話！

B: There is no doubt about it.

那是毫無疑問的。

應用會話

A: That's the stupidest thing I've ever heard.

那是我聽到最愚蠢的事！

B: There is no doubt about it.

那是毫無疑問的。

Track 101

很多事情的喜好是因人而異的，不用隱滿自己的喜好，不妨直接說明。

基礎對話

A: What do you think of it?

你覺得如何？

B: It sucks!

爛透了！

深入分析

What do you think of it?

你覺得如何？

詢問對方對某事物的意見，通常表示是否喜歡的意思。

應用會話

A: What do you think of it?

你覺得如何？

B: I'm crazy about it.

我很著迷。

應用會話

A: What do you think of it?

你覺得如何？

B: It's fantastic.

太棒了。

深入分析

It sucks!

爛透了！

表示很糟糕、令人不滿，是非常口語化說法，表達「爛透了」的意思。

應用會話

A: Well? How do you like it?

怎麼樣？你喜歡嗎？

B: It sucks!

爛透了！

應用會話

A: It sucks!

爛透了！

B: Oh, you don't like it.

喔，你不喜歡囉！

當你被冤枉時，請為自己的清白辯解，千萬不要讓自己變成冤大頭。

基礎對話

A: I'm innocent.

我是無辜的。

B: So what?

那又如何？

深入分析

I'm innocent.
我是無辜的。

表示自己是被誤會、揹了黑鍋的意思，innocent是無辜的意思。

應用會話

A: I'm innocent.

我是無辜的。

B: Who cares!

誰在乎啊！

應用會話

A: I'm innocent.

我是無辜的。

B: Yes, you are.

是的，你的確是！

深入分析

So what?

那又如何？

反問語氣，表示自己一點不在意，也就是要對方接受這個現狀的意思，帶有無奈的意味。

應用會話

A: Did you lose your mind?

你瘋啦？

B: So what?

那又如何？

應用會話

A: He'll teach you how to do it.

他會教你該怎麼做。

B: So what?

那又如何？

若是對對方的所為不滿，不用刻意隱瞞，而是要讓對方知道，才能有改進的空間。

基礎對話

A: Look what you did!
看看你做的好事！

B: I'll keep it a secret.
我會保守祕密的。

深入分析

Look what you did!
看看你做的好事！

表示要對方看看自己的作為，通常適用在負面的情境中。

應用會話

A: Look what you did !
看看你做的好事！

B: I didn't do anything wrong.
我沒做錯什麼事啊！

應用會話

A: Look what you did!

看看你做的好事！

B: I'm sorry. I didn't mean it.

對不起，我並沒有惡意。

深入分析

I'll keep it a secret.

我會保守祕密的。

keep it a secret表示「保持成為一個祕密」，也就是保守祕密，不洩漏口風的意思。

應用會話

A: I'll keep it a secret.

我會保守祕密的。

B: Will you?

你會嗎？

應用會話

A: I'll keep it a secret.

我會保守祕密的。

B: Come on !

你少來了！

若是有時間上的急迫壓力，就要記得說明，千萬不要因為不好意思說出口而延遲時間。

基礎對話

A: When do you want it?
你什麼時候要？

B: The sooner the better.
越快越好！

深入分析

When do you want it?
你什麼時候要？

通常表示希望對方告知自己，需要某物的時間期限，好讓自己能事先準備。

應用會話

A: When do you want it?
你什麼時候要？

B: Is tomorrow OK?
明天行嗎？

應用會話

A: When do you want it?

你什麼時候要？

B: By this Wednesday.

就這個星期三之前。

深入分析

The sooner the better.

越快越好！

表示時間緊急，希望事情處理的速度加快，也就是「越快越好」的意思。

應用會話

A: The sooner the better.

越快越好！

B: Sure.

好啊！

應用會話

A: The sooner the better.

越快越好！

B: No problem.

沒問題！

情境 105

Track 105

當犯錯時，該如何道歉甚至解釋清楚呢？

基礎對話

A: I may be wrong.
我可能錯了！

B: No wonder.
這就難怪了！

深入分析

I may be wrong.
我可能錯了！

表示承認自己可能解讀錯誤或做錯某事的意思，期望對方能原諒自己的錯誤。

應用會話

A: I may be wrong.
我可能錯了！

B: I don't care at all.
我一點都不在意。

應用會話

A: What are you trying to say?

你想要說什麼？

B: I may be wrong.

我可能錯了！

深入分析

No wonder.

這就難怪了！

表示符合自己先前的懷疑，並不為此感到意外的意思。

應用會話

A: No wonder.

這就難怪了！

B: About what?

關於什麼？

應用會話

A: I knew what happened between you and him.

我知道你和他之間發生了什麼事。

B: No wonder.

這就難怪了！

彼此之間若產生誤會，可要早一點解釋清楚，免得越描越黑啊！

基礎對話

A: How can you say that?
你怎麼能這麼說？

B: Don't get me wrong.
不要誤會我！

深入分析

How can you say that?
你怎麼能這麼說？

表示自己不理解對方為何會有如此言論的意思，帶有責問意味。

應用會話

A: How can you say that?
你怎麼能這麼說？

B: I didn't mean it.
我不是這個意思。

應用會話

A: How can you say that?

你怎麼能這麼說？

B: I don't care.

我不在意！

深入分析

Don't get me wrong.

不要誤會我！

字面意思是「不要把我弄錯」，也就是「不要誤會我」的意思。

應用會話

A: Don't get me wrong.

不要誤會我！

B: I don't want to talk about it.

我不想討論這件事。

應用會話

A: Don't get me wrong.

不要誤會我！

B: So what do you mean by that?

那你是什麼意思？

尷尬的狀況發生時，彼此該如何應對呢？以免後續的負面影響擴大！

基礎對話

A: I'm so embarrassed.
真的很不好意思！

B: Never mind.
沒關係啊！

深入分析

I'm so embarrassed.
真的很不好意思！

be embarrassed表示不好意思、過意不去的意思，表達自己羞愧的情境。

應用會話

A: I'm so embarrassed.
真的很不好意思！

B: You are?
你有嗎？

應用會話

A: Here you are again.

你又來了！

B: I'm so embarrassed.

真的很不好意思！

深入分析

Never mind.

沒關係啊！

表示自己不在意，也要對方不要放在心上，也帶有算了、不想討論的意思。

應用會話

A: I didn't bring enough cash.

我沒帶足夠的錢。

B: Never mind.

沒關係啊！

應用會話

A: I'm sorry to hear that.

我很遺憾聽見那件事。

B: Never mind.

沒關係啊！

電話用語有一定的基本禮貌，你知道要如何去電找人嗎？

基礎對話

A: Is Kenny in the office?
肯尼有在辦公室裡嗎？

B: Let me check it for you.
讓我為您查一下。

深入分析

Is Kenny in the office?
肯尼有在辦公室裡嗎？

電話用語，表示去電時要確認受話方是否在辦公室的意思。

應用會話

A: Is Kenny in the office?
肯尼有在辦公室裡嗎？

B: No, he's out for lunch.
沒有，他出去吃午餐了！

應用會話

A: Is Kenny in the office?

肯尼有在辦公室裡嗎？

B: Hold the line, please.

請稍等，別掛斷。

深入分析

Let me check it for you.

讓我為您查一下。

check something表示確認某事物的用語，常用 " check it for someone " 的句型。

應用會話

A: Do you have anyone like this?

你們有像這個的嗎？

B: Let me check it for you.

讓我為您查一下。

應用會話

A: It looks great. How much is it?

看起來不錯！這個賣多少錢？

B: Let me check it for you.

讓我為您查一下。

情境 109

當朋友之間有好東西要分享時，該如何說出口及禮貌應對呢？

基礎對話

A: I hope you like it.
希望你喜歡。

B: I do love it.
我的確很喜歡！

深入分析

I hope you like it.
希望你喜歡。

表示自己不確定對方喜歡或接受的程度，但誠心希望（hope）對方能喜歡。

應用會話

A: I hope you like it.
希望你喜歡。

B: You do?
你真的希望嗎？

應用會話

A: I hope you like it.

希望你喜歡。

B: Well, I don't like it.

嗯，我不喜歡耶！

深入分析

I do love it.
我的確很喜歡！

這裡的 " do+原形動詞 " 和疑問句無關，而是表示強調的立場表示「真的很...」的意思。

應用會話

A: How do you like it?

你喜歡嗎？

B: I do love it.

我的確很喜歡！

應用會話

A: I do love it.

我的確很喜歡！

B: I'm glad to hear that.

我很高興知道這件事。

情境 110

有時候人與人之間的相互吸引是沒有原因的，而當你不敢相信對方的言論時，該如何表示呢？

基礎對話

A: I'm attracted to Kenny.
我被肯尼深深吸引了。

B: Are you crazy?
你瘋啦？

深入分析

I'm attracted to Kenny.
我被肯尼深深吸引了。

" be attracted to someone " 表示深深被某人所吸引，可能因為對方的外表或個性等。

應用會話

A: Let's get it clear.
我們坦白地說吧！

B: OK. I'm attracted to Kenny.
好！我被肯尼深深吸引了。

應用會話

A: I'm attracted to Kenny.

我被肯尼深深吸引了。

B: What did you just say?

你剛剛說什麼？

深入分析

Are you crazy?
你瘋啦？

就和字面意思一樣，表示對方的行徑令人難以相信，甚至對方應該是「瘋了」才會這麼做！

應用會話

A: Are you crazy?

你瘋啦？

B: I am not.

我沒有！

應用會話

A: What do you say? Is it good or what?

你覺得如何呢？不錯吧？

B: Are you crazy?

你瘋啦？

個性若是好相處的人，通常人際關係也會比較好，你認同嗎？

基礎對話

A: Kenny is nice to everyone.
肯尼對大家都很友善！

B: Excuse me?
你說什麼？

深入分析

Kenny is nice to everyone.
肯尼對大家都很友善！

" be nice to someone " 表示對某人友善、和氣的意思。someone通常是受詞me、us、him、her、them或人名。

應用會話

A: What do you think of him?
你覺得他呢？

B: Kenny is nice to everyone.
肯尼對大家都很友善！

應用會話

A: She is nice to me.

她對我很友善！

B: Good.

那很好啊！

深入分析

Excuse me?

你說什麼？

表示自己沒聽清楚或不相信對方所言，希望對方再說一次的意思，通常使用疑問語氣。

應用會話

A: I am fired.

我被炒魷魚了！

B: Excuse me?

你說什麼？

應用會話

A: Excuse me?

你說什麼？

B: Never mind.

算了！

情境 112

想要邀約對方參加某個活動該如何開口？若得要拒絕又要如何開口呢？

基礎對話

A: Do you have any plans this weekend?
你這個週末有事嗎？

B: I have other plans.
我有其他計畫了！

深入分析

Do you have any plans this weekend?

你這個週末有事嗎？

Do you have any plans…通常是邀約的前言，表示是否已經有計畫（any plans）要做某事的意思，後面可以加某個時間點。

應用會話

A: Do you have any plans this weekend?
你這個週末有事嗎？

B: No, not at all. Why?
沒有，完全沒有！怎麼啦？

應用會話

A: Do you have any plans tonight?

你今晚有事嗎？

B: Yeah, I'm gonna visit one of my friends.

有啊！我要去拜訪我的一個朋友！

深入分析

I have other plans.

我有其他計畫了！

通常適用在對方有邀約，但你拒絕時的最佳理由，表示自己有安排其他事了。

應用會話

A: Let's go.

我們走吧！

B: Sorry, I have other plans.

抱歉，我有其他計畫了！

應用會話

A: I have other plans.

我有其他計畫了！

B: That's OK. Maybe some other time.

沒關係！那就下次再說吧！

良好的溝通的技巧，是應該彼此都能傾聽對方的意見。

基礎對話

A: What do you say?

你覺得如何呢？

B: Good. But not good enough.

不錯！但不夠好！

深入分析

What do you say?
你覺得如何呢？

當雙方討論彼此意見時，就應該先聽聽對方的想法。後面也可以加你提出的任何建議。

應用會話

A: What do you say we get out of here?

你覺得如何呢？我們出去走走！

B: I think it's good.

我覺得不錯！

A: What do you say?

你覺得如何呢？

B: I am sick of it.

我覺得煩透了！

深入分析

Good. But not good enough.

不錯！但不夠好！

讚美的技巧有很多種，not good enough表示不錯，但應該可以更好的鼓勵用語。

應用會話

A: Well?

怎麼樣呢？

B: Good. But not good enough.

不錯！但不夠好！

應用會話

A: Good. But not good enough.

不錯！但不夠好！

B: Why? What's the matter?

為什麼？怎麼了？

有話想說可不要悶在心裡喔，要大膽的表達自己的想法。

基礎對話

A: What's on your mind?
你在想什麼呢？

B: Nothing at all.
沒事啊！

深入分析

What's on your mind?
你在想什麼呢？

當對方若有所思時，你可以問問對方心裡（on your mind）在想什麼。

應用會話

A: What's on your mind?
你在想什麼呢？

B: I was wondering why she called me last night.
我在想昨晚她為什麼打電話給我。

應用會話

A: Hey, buddy, what's on your mind?

嘿，老兄，你心裡在想什麼？

B: About what?

關於什麼事？

深入分析

Nothing at all.

沒事啊！

nothing是個很多樣的回答用法，Nothing at all.表示啥事都沒發生的意思。

應用會話

A: Why? What's the matter?

為什麼？怎麼了？

B: Nothing at all.

沒事啊！

應用會話

A: What can I do for you?

我能為你做什麼？

B: Nothing at all.

都不需要！

當兩人中有一方較為強勢，便容易成為一言堂喔！

基礎對話

A: You are the boss.
你是老大，說了就算！

B: What can I say?
我能說什麼？

深入分析

You are the boss.
你是老大，說了就算！

表示自己只能聽從對方的想法，因為自己的輩份或階級不如對方的意思。

應用會話

A: I don't want to talk about it.
我不想討論這件事。

B: It's up to you. You are the boss.
由你決定！你說了就算！

應用會話

A: Is that clear?

夠清楚嗎？

B: You are the boss.

你是老大，說了就算！

深入分析

What can I say?

我能說什麼？

字面雖然是「我能說什麼」，但其實就是認同或不願評論的無奈意思。

應用會話

A: What can I say?

我能說什麼？

B: Nothing at all.

什麼都不要說！

應用會話

A: Any questions?

有任何問題嗎？

B: What can I say?

我能說什麼？

人際關係是平常就要用心經營的喔，讓對方感受你的誠意吧！

基礎對話

A: Can't you stay for dinner?
你不能留下來吃晚餐嗎？

B: I've got to go.
我必須要走了。

深入分析

Can't you stay for dinner?
你不能留下來吃晚餐嗎？

要如何表達自己的熱情？提出請對方留下來用餐是個良方喔！

應用會話

A: Can't you stay for dinner?
你不能留下來吃晚餐嗎？

B: I'd love to, but I can't.
我是很想，但沒辦法啊！

應用會話

A: Can't you stay for dinner?

你不能留下來吃晚餐嗎？

B: Tonight? Oh, no, I can't.

今晚？沒辦法啦！

深入分析

I've got to go.

我必須要走了。

表示自己非得要離開了，但是沒有說明原因。

應用會話

A: I've got to go.

我必須要走了。

B: See you.

再見囉！

應用會話

A: I've got to go.

我必須要走了。

B: Right now? It's only eight o'clock now.

現在？現在才八點鐘啊！

當不如意的事情發生時，彼此的相互依賴或是關心是很重要的。

基礎對話

A: We'll be fine.
我們會沒事的。

B: I hope so.
希望是這樣！

深入分析

We'll be fine.
我們會沒事的。

雖然有不好的事發生，但表示我們一切都會很好，也有希望對方不要擔心的意思。

應用會話

A: I'm sorry to hear that.
很抱歉聽到這個消息。

B: We'll be fine.
我們會沒事的。

應用會話

A: We'll be fine.

我們會沒事的。

B: Yeah?

是嗎？

深入分析

I hope so.

希望是這樣！

可以表示對對方的評論抱持懷疑，或結果有待觀察的意思。

應用會話

A: I hope so.

希望是這樣！

B: You really think so?

你真的這樣認為？

應用會話

A: It's no big deal.

這沒什麼大不了的。

B: I hope so.

希望是這樣！

情境 118

Track 118

事情的輕重緩急要如何界定？截止的時間是重要的判斷依據。

基礎對話

A: Can you finish it by three o'clock?
你能在三點鐘前完成嗎？

B: I'll do my best.
我盡量。

深入分析

Can you finish it by three o'clock?
你能在三點鐘前完成嗎？

設下截止時間（by+時間），才能讓對方有依循的標準喔！

應用會話

A: Can you finish it by three o'clock?
你能在三點鐘前完成嗎？

B: I'm afraid not.
恐怕不行。

應用會話

A: Can you finish it by five o'clock?

你能在五點鐘前完成嗎？

B: That's impossible.

不可能。

深入分析

I'll do my best.

我盡量。

表示自己不確定是否能做到某事，但會盡量做到的意思。

應用會話

A: I'll do my best.

我盡量。

B: Good.

很好！

應用會話

A: Would you do me a favor?

你能幫我一個忙嗎？

B: Sure. I'll do my best.

好啊！我盡量。

情境 119

Track 119

當彼此對某事的結論，是否同調？或是有天南地北的差異，要先確認一下喔！

基礎對話

A: It's for sure.
確定了！

B: Serious?
真的嗎？

深入分析

It's for sure.
確定了！

表示事情的發展結論幾乎已經確定了，並不容質疑的意思。

應用會話

A: It's for sure.
確定了！

B: Good to hear that.
很高興聽到你這麼說！

應用會話

A: It's for sure.

確定了！

B: I can't believe it.

真教人不敢相信！

深入分析

Serious?

真的嗎？

代表自己對所知悉的事感到不可思議、不相信，並向對方再三確認之意。

應用會話

A: Serious?

真的嗎？

A: Yeap. Why not?

是啊！為什麼不是？

應用會話

A: Serious?

真的嗎？

B: You really want to know the truth?

你真的想要知道真相？

幫忙是人們良性互動的基礎，千萬別忘記，助人為快樂之本喔！

基礎對話

A: Would you do me a favor?

你能幫我一個忙嗎？

B: I'll see what I can do.

我來看看我能幫什麼忙！

深入分析

Would you do me a favor?
你能幫我一個忙嗎？

do someone a favor就是幫某人的忙的意思，相同的意思也可以說give someone a hand。

應用會話

A: Would you do me a favor?

你能幫我一個忙嗎？

B: Sorry, I'm quite busy now.

抱歉，我現在很忙！

應用會話

A: Would you do me a favor?

你能幫我一個忙嗎？

B: Sure. What's up?

當然有啊！什麼事？

深入分析

I'll see what I can do.

我來看看我能幫什麼忙！

通常是回應對方提出幫忙的需求，表示自己會盡量協助的意思。

應用會話

A: I'll see what I can do.

我來看看我能幫什麼忙！

B: Thank you so much.

非常謝謝你！

應用會話

A: What do you say?

你覺得如何呢？

B: I'll see what I can do.

我來看看我能幫什麼忙！

情境 121

Track 121

很多事情不是三言兩語可以解釋清楚的，要有耐心聽完整件事的發展喔！

基礎對話

A: It's a long story.
說來話長。

B: Try me.
說來聽聽啊！

深入分析

It's a long story.
說來話長。

表示事情很冗長、很複雜，確認對方是否真的想要知道的意思。

應用會話

A: What happened to you?
你怎麼啦？

B: It's a long story.
說來話長。

應用會話

A: Are you guys OK?

你們大家還好吧？

B: It's a long story.

說來話長。

深入分析

Try me.

說來聽聽啊！

表示自己願意嘗試、接受，對方應該要給你機會知道的意思。

應用會話

A: It's not an easy job.

這件事不好處理！

B: Try me.

說來聽聽啊！

應用會話

A: Try me.

說來聽聽啊！

B: You really want to know?

你真的想要知道？

事情的複雜或難易程度，可不是一個人說了算的喔！

基礎對話

A: It's a piece of cake.
　太容易了。

B: It's hard to say.
　這很難說啊！

深入分析

It's a piece of cake.
太容易了。

表示事情實在是簡單到不行的意思，是一種自信可以處理好的言論。

應用會話

A: What do you say?
　你覺得呢？

B: It's a piece of cake.
　太容易了。

應用會話

A: Would you show me how to do it?

你能示範給我看如何作嗎？

B: Sure. A piece of cake!

當然好。這太簡單了！

深入分析

It's hard to say.
這很難說啊！

表示對方不應這麼快就下負面結論，是一種還有機會翻盤的用語。

應用會話

A: Don't you think so?

你不這樣認為嗎？

B: It's hard to say.

這很難說啊！

應用會話

A: It's hard to say.

這很難說啊！

B: Yeah, I think so.

是啊！我也是這樣認為！

情境 123

並不是每個人都有好能力，要秤秤自己斤兩，不要打腫臉充胖子啊！

基礎對話

A: I can't afford it.
我付不起。

B: It'll all work out.
事情會有辦法解決的。

深入分析

I can't afford it.
我付不起。

明白說出自己負擔不起某種經濟或財務的壓力。類似用法也可以用 " afford to +動名詞 " 的句型。

應用會話

A: I can't afford it.
我付不起。

B: What? Are you kidding me?
什麼啊？你在開我玩笑吧？

應用會話

A: I can't afford it.

我付不起。

B: So what?

那又怎麼樣？

深入分析

It'll all work out.

事情會有辦法解決的。

鼓勵對方，事情總會有辦法解決（work out）的意思。

應用會話

A: It'll all work out.

事情會有辦法解決的。

B: I hope so.

希望是這樣！

應用會話

A: It'll all work out.

事情會有辦法解決的。

B: I don't think so.

我不這麼認為！

當兩人對事件的發展結局有不同的論點，該如何達成共識？

基礎對話

A: It's going to happen.
事情百分百確定了。

B: Don't ever say that again.
不要再這麼說了！

深入分析

It's going to happen.
事情百分百確定了。

當事情的發展狀況，並不會令人感到意外時，就是結局囉！

應用會話

A: I don't think it's a good idea.
我覺得這不是一個好主意。

B: It's going to happen.
事情百分百確定了。

應用會話

A: It's going to happen.

事情百分百確定了。

B: Sure. What can we say?

當然啊！我們還能說什麼？

深入分析

Don't ever say that again.

不要再這麼說了！

不認同對方的言論，並希望對方不要再這麼說，直接否決此論點的意思。

應用會話

A: Don't ever say that again.

不要再這麼說了！

B: Why not?

為什麼不要？

應用會話

A: Don't ever say that again.

不要再這麼說了！

B: I have no choice.

我別無選擇啊！

情境 125

Track 125

事情的發展令人感到措手不及時，彼此該如何回應呢？

基礎對話

A: I don't know what to do.

我不知道要怎麼辦！

B: Don't panic.

不要慌張！

深入分析

I don't know what to do.

我不知道要怎麼辦！

表示自己無所從，有暗示對方協助，或希望能提供意見的意思。

應用會話

A: I don't know what to do.

我不知道要怎麼辦！

B: You have me.

你有我啊！

應用會話

A: What are you thinking about?

你在想什麼？

B: I don't know what to do.

我不知道要怎麼辦！

深入分析

Don't panic.
不要慌張！

安撫對方不要緊張，別因此亂了陣腳的意思。

應用會話

A: I can't solve this problem by myself.

我自己無法解決這個問題。

B: Don't panic.

不要慌張！

應用會話

A: Don't panic.

不要慌張！

B: I understand.

我瞭解！

當有不確定因素時，雙方應該就事件的發展好好討論的意思。

基礎對話

A: Is such a thing possible?
   這種事可能嗎？

B: No way!
   不可能！

深入分析

Is such a thing possible?
這種事可能嗎？

表示不確定此事（such a thing）是否有可能，也就是是否會發生的意思。

應用會話

A: Is such a thing possible?
   這種事可能嗎？

B: I don't think so.
   我不這麼認為。

應用會話

A: Is such a thing possible?

這種事可能嗎？

B: What do you say?

你覺得呢？

深入分析

No way!

不可能！

表示一切都是不可能發生，是一種斬釘截鐵的否認回應。

應用會話

A: Can you cover it for me?

可以幫我掩護一下嗎？

B: No way!

不可能！

應用會話

A: Can you help me with this?

可以幫我這個忙嗎？

B: No way!

不可能！

雖然眼見不一定為憑，但是還是要再確認是否有其他的目擊者。

基礎對話

A: Did anybody else see it?
還有其他人看到嗎？

B: No one saw it but me.
除了我沒以外，沒人看到。

深入分析

Did anybody else see it?
還有其他人看到嗎？

想到知道是否還有其他人或第三方（anybody else）目擊某事的意思，通常用過去式語句。

應用會話

A: Did anybody else see it?
還有其他人看到嗎？

B: I don't think so.
我不這麼認為。

應用會話

A: Did anybody else see it?
還有其他人看到嗎？

B: Yes, Kenny saw it.
有的，肯尼有看到！

深入分析

No one saw it but me.
除了我沒以外，沒人看到。

表示自己是某事件的唯一目擊者。

應用會話

A: No one saw it but me.
除了我沒以外，沒人看到。

B: Good. Just tell me the truth.
很好！那就只要告訴我事實！

應用會話

A: Someone saw it?
有人有看見嗎？

B: No one saw it but me.
除了我沒以外，沒人看到。

若是要討論不在場的第三方，彼此都應該開誠布公地說出想法。

基礎對話

A: You really don't want to see her, do you?
你真的不想見到她，對吧？

B: If possible.
如果可能的話！

深入分析

You really don't want to see her, do you?

你真的不想見到她，對吧？

表示要確認對方不願見到某一女性（her）的意思，若是某男性則用him。也可以直接用人名替代，或是第三人稱的them。

應用會話

A: You really don't want to see her, do you?
你真的不想見到她，對吧？

B: What makes you think so?
你為什麼會這麼認為？

應用會話

A: You really don't want to see them, do you?

你真的不想見到他們，對吧？

B: That's true.

是真的！

深入分析

If possible.

如果可能的話！

雖不是完整的句子，但是表示認同對方之前的某個言論的意思。

應用會話

A: You won't let it happen again, right?

你決不允許這件事再發生，對吧？

B: If possible.

如果可能的話！

應用會話

A: Would you like to see the black ones?

你要看看黑色的嗎？

B: Yes, please, if possible.

如果可能的話，麻煩你囉！

雙方應該就可能產生誤會的事，查出真相！

基礎對話

A: Nobody told me anything.

沒人告訴我任何事。

B: I thought you knew it.

我以為你知道！

深入分析

Nobody told me anything.
沒人告訴我任何事。

表示自己一無所知，是因為沒有被告知，也無人提及此事的意思。

應用會話

A: Nobody told me anything.

沒人告訴我任何事。

B: That wasn't weird.

那不奇怪啊！

應用會話

A: Nobody told me anything.

沒人告訴我任何事。

B: Really? How strange!

真的？好奇怪呀！

深入分析

I thought you knew it.

我以為你知道！

表示自己以為對方是知道某事的意思。

應用會話

A: What happened?

發生了什麼事？

B: I thought you knew it.

我以為你知道！

應用會話

A: I thought you knew it.

我以為你知道！

B: About what?

有關什麼事？

提出需求與回應需求的用語，只要一句話就可以完成。

基礎對話

A: Please give me a new one.

請給我一個新的！

B: Sure, right away.

好，馬上就來。

深入分析

Please give me a new one.
請給我一個新的！

希望對方能再提供某物，而且是全新或乾淨、無損壞的意思，通常是因為你自己手上這個不堪使用了。

應用會話

A: May I help you?

需要我效勞嗎？

B: Yes. Please give me a new one.

是的！請給我一個新的！

應用會話

A: Please give me a new one.

請給我一個新的！

B: No problem, sir.

好的，先生。

深入分析

Sure, right away.

好，馬上就來。

回應用語，表示自己會馬上（right away）處理的意思。

應用會話

A: May I have another piece of cake?

可以再給我一片蛋糕嗎？

B: Sure, right away.

好，馬上就來。

應用會話

A: Can you send someone up here?

可以派個人上來嗎？

B: Sure, right away.

好，馬上就來。

情境 131

Track 131

事情的發展，一方提出定論，另一方有肯定與否定的回應。

基礎對話

A: It wasn't too bad.
　不嚴重啦！

B: I agree.
　我同意。

深入分析

It wasn't too bad.

不嚴重啦！

表示事情並不會太糟糕，也有讓對方不用再擔心的意思。

應用會話

A: Oh, my.
　喔！我的天啊！

B: It wasn't too bad, right?
　不差，對吧？

應用會話

A: It wasn't too bad.

不嚴重啦！

B: I think so, too.

我也是這麼想。

深入分析

I agree.
我同意。

表示同意對方的評論，若不同意，則為I don't agree。

應用會話

A: It is not so easy as we think.

這事沒有我們想像的那麼簡單。

B: I agree.

我同意。

應用會話

A: It really takes time.

這樣太耽誤時間了。

B: I agree.

我同意。

情境
132

Track 132

顧客與服務生之間的點餐對談，該如何進行？

基礎對話

A: I'd like a cup of tea, please.

我要喝一杯茶，謝謝。

B: Here you are.

來，給你！

深入分析

I'd like a cup of tea, please.
我要喝一杯茶，謝謝。

直接說明自己想要喝茶的意思，後面的please有謝謝你、麻煩你之意。

應用會話

A: What would you like to drink, coffee or tea?

你想喝什麼，咖啡還是茶？

B: I'd like a cup of tea, please.

我要喝一杯茶，謝謝。

應用會話

A: Can I get you something?

要我幫你準備什麼嗎？

B: I'd like a cup of tea, please.

我要喝一杯茶，謝謝。

深入分析

Here you are.

來，給你！

拿某物給對方時隨口的用語，就是中文的「拿去」、「給你」。

應用會話

A: Pass me the salt, please.

請把鹽巴遞給我！

B: Here you are.

來，給你！

應用會話

A: Here you are.

來，給你！

B: Thank you so much.

非常謝謝你！

Track 133

休息是為了走更長遠的路，經過一天的操勞，該是休息的時候到了。

基礎對話

A: I'm so tired.
我好累喔！

B: Let's call it a day.
今天就告一個段落吧！

深入分析

I'm so tired.
我好累喔！

表示自己已經疲累、體力不支，有希望能休息的意思。

應用會話

A: I'm so tired.
我好累喔！

B: Why don't you take a break?
你怎麼不休息一下？

應用會話

A: You look awful.

你看起來糟透了！

B: Yeap, I'm so tired.

是啊！我好累喔！

深入分析

Let's call it a day.

今天就告一個段落吧！

表示今天的事情可以告一段落了，應該先休息，明天再繼續的意思。

應用會話

A: Let's call it a day.

今天就告一個段落吧！

B: Good. Let's go home.

好！我們回家吧！

應用會話

A: Let's call it a day.

今天就告一個段落吧！

B: Are you sure?

你確定嗎？

休息是為了走更長遠的路，該休息就不要硬撐喔！

基礎對話

A: Let's take a break.
　我們休息一會兒。

B: Time is running out!
　沒有時間了！

深入分析

Let's take a break.
我們休息一會兒。

take a break是稍事休息，或暫時中斷片刻，以休息的意思。

應用會話

A: Let's take a break.
　我們休息一會兒。

B: Sure. Want some coffee?
　好啊！要喝咖啡嗎？

應用會話

A: Let's take a break.

我們休息一會兒。

B: Good idea!

好主意！

深入分析

Time is running out!
沒有時間了！

表示時間不夠了（run out），希望相關人員能加緊腳步、繼續加油的意思。

應用會話

A: Time is running out!

沒有時間了！

B: I don't care.

我不在意！

應用會話

A: How much time do we have now?

我們現在有多少時間？

B: Time is running out!

沒有時間了！

一夜狂歡、飲酒作樂之後，會有哪些後遺症？面對這樣的人，你會有何種反應？

基礎對話

A: I had a terrible hangover after the party.
在派對後，我宿醉得十分難受。

B: I can expect it.
我想也是！

深入分析

I had a terrible hangover after the party.

在派對後，我宿醉得十分難受。

hangover是宿醉、不舒服的意思。

應用會話

A: Are you OK?
你還好吧？

B: I had a terrible hangover after the party.
在派對後，我宿醉得十分難受。

應用會話

A: What's the matter?

怎麼啦？

B: I had a terrible hangover after the party.

在派對後，我宿醉得十分難受。

深入分析

I can expect it.

我想也是！

表示和自己預期的一樣，也就是對結論不會感到意外的回應。

應用會話

A: David and I haven't seen each other lately.

我和大衛最近沒有見面。

B: I can expect it.

我想也是！

應用會話

A: He's not available at the moment.

他現在有沒有空。

B: I can expect it.

我想也是！

情境 136

不認同對方的態度或行為時，要如何表達你的立場呢？而當事人該如何為自己辯駁？

基礎對話

A: Don't be such a chicken.
不要像個膽小鬼一樣！

B: I can't help it.
我無法自制啊！

深入分析

Don't be such a chicken.
不要像個膽小鬼一樣！

希望對方能勇敢一些，不要不敢面對問題的意思。chicken是雞的意思，但也有膽小鬼之意。

應用會話

A: Don't be such a chicken.
不要像個膽小鬼一樣！

B: Why not?
為什麼不可以？

應用會話

A: Don't be such a chicken.

不要像個膽小鬼一樣！

B: Sure.

當然啊！

深入分析

I can't help it.

我無法自制啊！

表示自己也不願意這樣，但是就是無法自我控制（行為、思想或言語）的意思。

應用會話

A: I can't help it.

我無法自制啊！

B: About what?

關於什麼事無法克制？

應用會話

A: Don't do this.

不要這麼做！

B: I can't help it.

我無法自制啊！

沒有兩人天生想法就能一致，雙方就某事的評論，要如何達成共識？

基礎對話

A: It means nothing.
沒啥意義！

B: Yeah, it is.
是啊！的確如此！

深入分析

It means nothing.
沒啥意義！

表示對於某事感到無所謂、不重要就是nothing，也可表示無意義的意思。

應用會話

A: It means nothing.
沒啥意義！

B: I can't believe what you just said.
我不敢相信你剛剛說的！

應用會話

A: It means nothing.

沒啥意義！

B: I don't think so.

我不這麼認為！

深入分析

Yeah, it is.

是啊！的確如此！

表示深刻認同，特別是對方對於某事的評論。不可以用縮寫it's表示，以表示強調。

應用會話

A: It's all past.

事情都都過去了。

B: Yeah, it is.

是啊！的確如此！

應用會話

A: Maybe it's some kind of personal problem.

也許就是些個人的問題！

B: Yeah, it is.

是啊！的確如此！

冷漠是很多人的常態行為，但是應該先管好自己的事吧！

基礎對話

A: It's somebody else's problem.
那是別人家的事。

B: Mind your own business.
別多管閒事！

深入分析

It's somebody else's problem.
那是別人家的事。

表示某事是第三方以外的他人事件，不用對方多操心的意思。

應用會話

A: You can't get away with it.
你無法置身事外。

B: It's somebody else's problem.
那是別人家的事。

應用會話

A: What are you going to do?

你打算要怎麼處理？

B: It's somebody else's problem.

那是別人家的事。

深入分析

Mind your own business.
別多管閒事！

希望對方不要管閒事，也不必太操心他人的事的意思。

應用會話

A: Are you dating?

你們兩人在交往嗎？

B: Mind your own business.

別多管閒事！

應用會話

A: Are you on the net again?

你又在上網了？

B: Mind your own business.

別多管閒事！

人是互助的社會群體，當對方有困難，你要如何安慰、回應呢？

基礎對話

A: It's not easy for you.
難為你了！

B: Could you give me an idea for it?
你能給我建議？

深入分析

It's not easy for you.
難為你了！

表示對方所經歷的這一切，一定是很難受（not easy）實在令人同情的意思。

應用會話

A: It's not easy for you.
難為你了！

B: Do you have any idea?
你有任何的意見嗎？

應用會話

A: It's not easy for you.
難為你了！

B: Don't worry about me.
不用擔心我！

深入分析

Could you give me an idea for it?
你能給我建議？

希望對方能提供意見，幫助自己度過難關的意思。

應用會話

A: Could you give me an idea for it?
你能給我建議？

B: Don't expect me to help you out.
別指望我幫你解決問題。

應用會話

A: Could you give me an idea for it?
你能給我建議？

B: Don't take it so hard.
看開一點！

情境 140

Track 140

某事的發展若是不如意時，彼此都有權提出自己的評論。

基礎對話

A: Can't you do anything right?
你真是成事不足，敗事有餘！

B: It's not the point.
這不是重點。

深入分析

Can't you do anything right?
你真是成事不足，敗事有餘！

表示對方沒有一件事有做好（do anything right）的意思。

應用會話

A: Can't you do anything right?
你真是成事不足，敗事有餘！

B: Enough!
夠了！

應用會話

A: Can't you do anything right?
你真是成事不足，敗事有餘！

B: Are you done?
你說完了嗎？

深入分析

It's not the point.
這不是重點。

表示對方的言論已經失去焦點，只是蒜皮小事的意思。

應用會話

A: Face it.
你應該要面對現實！

B: It's not the point.
這不是重點。

應用會話

A: Forgive me, but you are wrong.
原諒我的指責，但是你錯了。

B: It's not the point.
這不是重點。

雖說人們應該彼此互動，但幫忙與否，端看彼此的意願與需求喔！

基礎對話

A: Hi, can I help you?
　嗨，需要我的幫忙嗎？

B: I'm afraid not.
　恐怕不可以！

深入分析

Hi, can I help you?
嗨，需要我的幫忙嗎？

直接詢問對方，是否需要協助的意思。

應用會話

A: Hi, can I help you?
　嗨，需要我的幫忙嗎？

B: Yes, please.
　好的，麻煩你了！

應用會話

A: Hi, can I help you?

嗨，需要我的幫忙嗎？

B: No, thanks.

不必麻煩了！

深入分析

I'm afraid not.

恐怕不可以！

非直接拒絕，而是具有暗示意味，表示否定的意思，帶有很抱歉事情如此的意味。

應用會話

A: Can you break a twenty-dollar bill?

你能找得開廿元的鈔票嗎？

B: I'm afraid not.

恐怕不可以！

應用會話

A: Can you do the dishes?

你可以洗碗嗎？

B: I'm afraid not.

恐怕不可以！

情境 142

表示彼此雙方的關係，是建立在提供與接受的關係。

基礎對話

A: And you?
你呢？

B: Coffee, please.
請給我咖啡。

深入分析

And you?
你呢？

通常是詢問過某一方後，再向第三方確認同樣問題的意思，後方可接尊稱對方的敬詞，如sir或是madam。

應用會話

A: I would like a cup of black tea.
我要點一杯紅茶。

B: OK. A cup of black tea. And you, sir?
好的，一杯紅茶。先生，那您呢？

C: Coffee, please.
請給我咖啡。

應用會話

A: And you, madam?

女士，您呢？

B: No, thanks.

我不用，謝謝！

深入分析

Coffee, please.

請給我咖啡。

直接說明自己想要的飲料名稱的用語，後面的please有表示麻煩你了之意。

應用會話

A: What about you?

你呢？

B: Coffee, please.

請給我咖啡。

應用會話

A: What do you want to drink?

你想喝什麼？

B: Just water, please.

請給我水就好。

情境 143

Track 143

好運氣人人都需要，該如何送出你的祝福呢？

基礎對話

A: Good luck to you.
祝你好運。

B: I really need it.
我真的需要有好運氣。

深入分析

Good luck to you.
祝你好運。

對於即將有考試或難關要過的人來說，絕對需要你的好運祝福的。也可以只是說Good luck。

應用會話

A: I'm going to take the written test tomorrow.
我明天要參加筆試。

B: Good luck to you, David.
大衛，祝你好運。

A: Thanks. I really need it.
謝謝，我真的需要有好運氣。

應用會話

A: Good luck.

祝好運！

B: Yeah, you too.

是啊！你也是！

深入分析

I really need it.

我真的需要。

表示強調自己的確需要對方提及的某物的回應。

應用會話

A: Good luck to you.

祝你好運。

B: Yeah, I really need it.

是啊！我真的需要有好運氣！

應用會話

A: Here you are.

給你！

B: Thanks. I really need it.

謝謝！我真的需要。

要想和他人討論之前，先確認彼此是否都有空吧！

基礎對話

A: Got a minute?
現在有空嗎？

B: What do you want?
你想怎麼樣？

深入分析

Got a minute?
現在有空嗎？

字面是有沒有一分鐘，也就是和對方確認是否有空講話的意思。

應用會話

A: Got a minute?
現在有空嗎？

B: I'm afraid not.
恐怕沒空！

應用會話

A: Got a minute?

現在有空嗎？

B: What's up?

有什麼事？

深入分析

What do you want?

你想怎麼樣？

直接詢問對方想要做什麼事或有何打算的意思。

應用會話

A: What do you want?

你想怎麼樣？

B: Nothing. Don't worry about me.

沒事！不要擔心我啦！

應用會話

A: Can I talk to you?

我能和你聊一聊嗎？

B: What do you want?

你想怎麼樣？

情境 145

Track 145

評論對方，不需要太多的言語就能辦到，但要注意語氣喔！

基礎對話

A: Look at you.
看看你！

B: I don't mind.
我不在意！

深入分析

Look at you.
看看你！

字面意思是看看你，也帶有目前你很糟糕、怎麼把自己搞成這樣的評論的意思 。

應用會話

A: Look at you. What happened to you?
看看你！你怎麼了？

B: David punched me last night.
大衛昨晚打我！

應用會話

A: Look at you.

看看你！

B: I am fine.

我很好啊！

深入分析

I don't mind.

我不在意！

表示自己是不在意、不在乎的怡然自得的心態。

應用會話

A: It's going to happen.

但事情已經百分百確定了。

B: So what? I don't mind.

那又怎樣？我不在意！

應用會話

A: It's so hard for you.

這對你來說真是難熬。

B: I don't mind.

我不在意！

當不認同對方所表示的期待值，該如何表示你的提醒立場呢？

基礎對話

A: I look forward to it.
我很期待這件事。

B: You will be sorry.
你會後悔的！

深入分析

I look forward to it.
我很期待這件事。

表示自己對於某事（it），很期待（look forward to）發生或到來的意思，it的後方可接名詞或動詞。

應用會話

A: Are you going to Tom's birthday party?
你有要去參加湯姆的生日派對嗎？

B: Of course. I look forward to it.
當然！我很期待這件事。

應用會話

A: I look forward to seeing her.

我很期待見到她。

B: Me too.

我也是啊！

深入分析

You will be sorry.

你會後悔的！

提醒、警告對方可能會面臨後悔的窘境，希望對方能夠注意的意思。

應用會話

A: I quit.

我不幹了！

B: You will be sorry.

你會後悔的！

應用會話

A: You will be sorry.

你會後悔的！

B: Whatever!

管他的！

事情的發展都是千變萬化的，很難有個定論！

基礎對話

A: It's so confusing.
事情實在啟人疑竇。

B: Say no more.
不要再說了！

深入分析

It's so confusing.
事情實在啟人疑竇。

表示雙方所討論的某事，令人感到懷疑的意思。confusing是形容事情令人糊塗，若是形容人，則用I'm confused。

應用會話

A: It's so confusing.
事情實在啟人疑竇。

B: You still didn't get it?
你還是沒弄懂？

應用會話

A: It's so confusing.

事情實在啟人疑竇。

B: It can't be.

怎麼可能！

深入分析

Say no more.

不要再說了！

表示自己不想再聽，要對方住口的意思。

應用會話

A: I saw your wife went to see a movie with Kenny.

我看見你太太和肯尼去看電影。

B: Say no more.

不要再說了！

應用會話

A: Say no more.

不要再說了！

B: No problem.

沒問題！

情境 148

Track 148

觀念不同的雙方，若無良性的溝通方式，可是很容易起衝突！

基礎會話

A: It's too good to be true.
哪有這麼好的事？

B: What do you mean by that?
你這是什麼意思？

深入分析

It's too good to be true.
哪有這麼好的事？

表示某件事實在是好的令人不敢相信的意思。too...to表示「太...以致於...」否定之意。

應用會話

A: It's too good to be true.
哪有這麼好的事？

B: Kind of.
有一點。

應用會話

A: I won the lottery twice.

我中了兩次彩券。

B: It's too good to be true.

哪有這麼好的事？

深入分析

What do you mean by that?

你這是什麼意思？

可能是對話方說了某件事（by that），而你不懂，想要確認對方的說詞的意思。

應用會話

A: What do you mean by that?

你這是什麼意思？

B: Nothing!

什麼事都沒有啊！

應用會話

A: What do you mean by that?

你這是什麼意思？

B: Well, it's only a matter of taste.

哦，這只是品味的問題。

若是兩人因意見不同而起了爭執，千萬不要輕易動怒喔！

基礎對話

A: It's shame on you.
你太丟臉了。

B: Leave me alone.
不要管我！

深入分析

It's shame on you.
你太丟臉了。

認為對方的某些言行令人感到丟臉、羞愧（shame）的意思。

應用會話

A: It's shame on you.
你太丟臉了。

B: Give me a break.
饒了我吧！

應用會話

A: I quit.

我不想幹了！

B: It's shame on you.

你太丟臉了。

深入分析

Leave me alone.

不要管我！

不管如何，希望對方不要再來騷擾或關心自己，希望自己可以獨處的意思。

應用會話

A: You can't do anything now.

你現在不能做任何事。

B: Leave me alone.

不要管我！

應用會話

A: Leave me alone.

不要管我！

B: Sure!

好啊！

當對方有所抱怨或認為事情屬於不可能時，你該如何應對對方的抱怨立場？

基礎對話

A: It's impossible.
不可能！

B: You can't complain.
你該知足了！

深入分析

It's impossible.
不可能！

對於不敢相信的事，採取不認同的立場時，就可以說 impossible。

應用會話

A: It's impossible.
不可能！

B: Ah-huh, you'll get used to it.
啊哈！你會習慣的！

應用會話

A: It's impossible.

不可能！

B: Take it or leave it.

要就接受，不然拉倒！

深入分析

You can't complain.
你該知足了！

面對一個老是抱怨的人，你可以告訴對方要適可而止。

應用會話

A: I don't want this.

我不要這樣！

B: You can't complain.

你該知足了！

應用會話

A: You can't complain.

你該知足了！

B: Why not?

為什麼不可以？

面對一些小道消息，該如何謠言止於智者或相信這一切呢？

基礎對話

A: Someone has a crush on Penny.
有人對潘妮很著迷。

B: Never heard of that!
沒聽說過！

深入分析

Someone has a crush on Penny.
有人對潘妮很著迷。

have a crush on someone表示對某人有愛慕之意的意思，通常是男女之情的情愫。

應用會話

A: Someone has a crush on Penny.
有人對潘妮很著迷。

B: Who has a crush?
誰著迷？

應用會話

A: Someone has a crush on him.

有人對他很著迷。

B: On David? No way!

對大衛？不會吧！

深入分析

Never heard of that!

沒聽說過！

表示對方所說的這件事，對你來說是新鮮事，也就是沒有聽過的意思。

應用會話

A: You know what? Kenny is a jerk.

你知道嗎？肯尼是個混蛋！

B: Never heard of that!

沒聽說過！

應用會話

A: Never heard of that!

沒聽說過！

B: It's the truth.

這就是事實！

面對問題，大家都希望能夠盡快解決，提出建議總比放任不管來得好！

基礎對話

A: Say something.
說說話吧！

B: Don't look at me.
不要看我！

深入分析

Say something.
說說話吧！

字面意思是要對方說話，也就是暗示對方提出解決辦法的意思。

應用會話

A: Say something.
說說話吧！

B: I have nothing to say.
我無話可說！

應用會話

A: Say something.

說說話吧！

B: I know nothing about it.

我什麼都不知道啊！

深入分析

Don't look at me.

不要看我！

字面意思是不要看我，其實是撇清責任或捍衛清白，表示事不關己的意思。

應用會話

A: Who did this?

這是誰幹的好事？

B: Don't look at me.

不要看我！

應用會話

A: Don't look at me.

不要看我！

B: Easy!

放輕鬆啊！

一個要耳根清淨，但面對另一個喜歡囉唆的人，雙方該如何相處？

基礎對話

A: That is life.
人生就是這樣！

B: Are you done?
你說完了嗎？

深入分析

That is life.
人生就是這樣！

人生不一定苦短，但有一些人生難關，天生就會存在的，這就是人生，有要對方認清事實之意。

應用會話

A: That is life.
人生就是這樣！

B: What are you talking about?
你在說什麼啊！

應用會話

A: That is life.

人生就是這樣！

B: I agree.

我同意！

深入分析

Are you done?

你說完了嗎？

字面意思是做完了嗎，其實是要對方住嘴、不要再說的意思。

應用會話

A: Don't be such a jerk.

不要像個混蛋！

B: Are you done?

你說完了嗎？

應用會話

A: Don't give me a look like that.

不要給我這種表情！

B: Are you done?

你說完了嗎？

人生永遠充滿機會，如果一個不願嘗試的人，是永遠無法出頭天！

基礎對話

A: Let me try.
我來試一下！

B: It's your choice.
這是你的抉擇。

深入分析

Let me try.
我來試一下！

希望對方給自己機會嘗試的意思，是不願放棄、尋找機會之意！

應用會話

A: Let me try.
我來試一下！

B: Go ahead.
去吧！

應用會話

A: Let me try.

我來試一下！

B: No, you can't.

不，你不可以！

深入分析

It's your choice.

這是你的抉擇。

也許不是最好的決定，卻是對方的抉擇的意思，表示決定權在對方之意。

應用會話

A: We're gonna travel around the world.

我們要去環遊世界！

B: It's your choice.

這是你的抉擇。

應用會話

A: Don't tell her. I want it to be a surprise.

不要告訴她。我要讓她驚喜一下。

B: OK, it's your choice.

好吧，這是你的抉擇。

當發生不可思議的事情時，該如何表示自己不相信的驚訝立場？

基礎對話

A: Uh, no!
喔，不會吧？

B: I have no choice.
我別無選擇啊！

深入分析

Uh, no!
喔，不會吧？

在這裡不是拒絕，而是類似中文「不會吧！」的不相信口吻。

應用會話

A: Uh, no!
喔，不會吧？

B: Believe me. It's true.
相信我！是真的！

應用會話

A: See? I told you so.

看吧！我告訴過你啊！

B: Uh, no!

喔，不會吧？

深入分析

I have no choice.

我別無選擇啊！

表示自己是迫於無奈下的決定或選擇。no choice就是沒得選擇之意。

應用會話

A: I'm so disappointed.

我很失望。

B: I have no choice.

我別無選擇啊！

應用會話

A: Shame on you.

你真丟臉！

B: I have no choice.

我別無選擇啊！

提出警告是身為朋友的責任，但對方若是不聽從，該怎麼辦？

基礎對話

A: See? Didn't I tell you so?
看吧！我不是告訴過你嗎？

B: What shall I do now?
我現在該怎麼辦？

深入分析

See? Didn't I tell you so?
看吧！我不是告訴過你嗎？

不是要對方看，而是再次提醒自己曾經警告過對方某事（tell you so）的意思。

應用會話

A: See? Didn't I tell you so?
看吧！我不是告訴過你嗎？

B: I'm terribly sorry.
我真的很抱歉！

應用會話

A: What a mess over here.

這裡真是一團亂！

B: See? Didn't I tell you so?

看吧！我不是告訴過你嗎？

深入分析

What shall I do now?

我現在該怎麼辦？

面對問題不知道該如何應對，希望對方給自己幫助的意思。

應用會話

A: What shall I do now?

我現在該怎麼辦？

B: You tell me.

你說呢？

應用會話

A: What shall I do now?

我現在該怎麼辦？

B: I have no idea.

我不知道。

國家圖書館出版品預行編目資料

OK, no problem你一定要會的基礎對話 / 張瑜凌 編著.
-- 初版. -- 新北市 : 雅典文化, 民101.11
面 ; 公分. -- (全民學英文 ; 29)
ISBN 978-986-6282-68-3(平裝附光碟片)
1.英語 2.會話
805.188 101018184

全民學英文系列 29

OK, no problem. 你一定要會的基礎對話

編　　著／張瑜凌
責　　編／張瑜凌
美術編輯／林于婷
封面設計／劉　基

法律顧問：方圓法律事務所／涂成樞律師

總經銷：永續圖書有限公司
永續圖書線上購物網
www.foreverbooks.com.tw

CVS代理／美璟文化有限公司
TEL：（02）2723-9968
FAX：（02）2723-9668

出版日／2012年11月

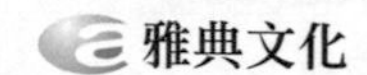

出版社
22103 新北市汐止區大同路三段194號9樓之1
TEL （02）8647-3663
FAX （02）8647-3660

全民學英文
29

OK,no problem. 你一定要會的基礎對話

雅致風靡　典藏文化

親愛的顧客您好，感謝您購買這本書。即日起，填寫讀者回函卡寄回至本公司，我們每月將抽出一百名回函讀者，寄出精美禮物並享有生日當月購書優惠！想知道更多更即時的消息，歡迎加入"永續圖書粉絲團"
您也可以選擇傳真、掃描或用本公司準備的免郵回函寄回，謝謝。

傳真電話：（02）8647-3660　　電子信箱：yungjiuh@ms45.hinet.net

姓名：　　性別：　□男　□女

出生日期：　年　月　日　電話：

學歷：　　職業：　□男　□女

E-mail：

地址：□□□

從何處購買此書：　　購買金額：　元

購買本書動機：□封面 □書名 □排版 □內容 □作者 □偶然衝動

你對本書的意見：
內容：□滿意□尚可□待改進　編輯：□滿意□尚可□待改進
封面：□滿意□尚可□待改進　定價：□滿意□尚可□待改進

其他建議：

您可以使用以下方式將回函寄回。

您的回覆，是我們進步的最大動力，謝謝。

① 使用本公司準備的免郵回函寄回。

② 傳真電話：（02）8647-3660

③ 掃描圖檔寄到電子信箱：

yungjiuh@ms45.hinet.net

沿此線對折後寄回，謝謝。

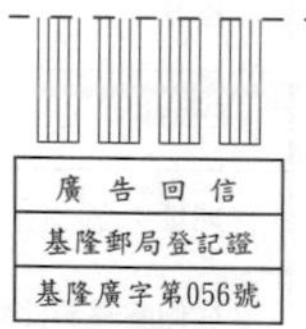

221-03

雅典文化事業有限公司　收

新北市汐止區大同路三段194號9樓之1

雅致風靡　典藏文化